Ittehad

Women Translating Women
A collaborative project of the Ashoka Centre for Translation, the Susham Bedi Memorial Fund and Zubaan Publishers

The Ashoka Centre for Translation, through its initiatives, is committed to thinking about translation from a many-to-many perspective to foster India's multilingual ethos. The Women Translating Women project, under which this book has been supported, is a joint initiative of the Centre and the Susham Bedi Memorial Fund. The Fund, established in memory of the Hindi poet and author Susham Bedi (1 July 1945–20 March 2020), supports the publication of 12 books over two years by Zubaan Publishers.

translation.ashoka.edu.in
sushambedi.com
zubaanbooks.com

Ittehad

A Life Together

Guli Sadarangani

Translated and with an introduction by Rita Kothari

zubaan

ZUBAAN
128 B Shahpur Jat, 1st floor
NEW DELHI 110 049
Email: contact@zubaanbooks.com
Website: www.zubaanbooks.com

First published by Zubaan Publishers Pvt. Ltd 2025

10 9 8 7 6 5 4 3 2 1

ISBN 978 81 98792 70 9 (paperback)
ISBN 978 81 98792 73 0 (ebook)

Zubaan is an independent feminist publishing house based in New Delhi with a strong academic and general list. It was set up as an imprint of India's first feminist publishing house, Kali for Women, and carries forward Kali's tradition of publishing world quality books to high editorial and production standards. *Zubaan* means tongue, voice, language, speech in Hindustani. Zubaan publishes in the areas of the humanities, social sciences, as well as in fiction, general non-fiction, and books for children and young adults under its Young Zubaan imprint.

Typeset in Sabon 11/16.
Printed and bound at Chaman Enterprises.

Preface to the 1st Edition, 1941

An original is always better than its copy—this has been my conviction for years. However, the difference between an original and its replication only became fully clear to me while I was writing *Ittehad.* When I translated Jawaharlal Nehru's letters to his daughter and Rabindranath Tagore's *Gora* in Sindhi, I felt immense happiness. However, the happiness I experienced while writing *Ittehad* was something beyond words. It is like the indescribable feeling of holding your newborn baby—that's what writing your own book feels like. A *parai* or someone else's book cannot give you the same sense of joy. What a mother feels while holding her own baby is something a nurse, despite her care and nurturing, could never experience with someone else's child.

The pitfalls of Indian society, such as the exploitation of the poor by the rich, the oppression of women by men, and the atrocities of caste, fill me with despair. God knows when our country will cease to be enslaved by such oppression. In the name of dharma or religion, lawlessness prevails. I feel we are descending into an abyss. What do we even mean by religion? Things that cause damage and actions that are inimical to religion, we define as religious and fan animosities. Honestly, the Hindu is bringing a bad name to his religion and the Muslim to his. Stalwarts like the great poet Tagore, Sri Aurobindo, and Mahatma Gandhi understood religion more deeply than most, don't you agree? They have grasped the essence of all religions and philosophies. They do not teach us to practice discrimination against other religions and castes. Tagore's ashram is inhabited by Harijans, Hindus, Muslims, Parsis, Christians, etc. All of them coexist and mingle with each other. Only those are considered superior who have higher thinking and bigger hearts. Truly, if different communities are to live with mutual respect and harmony, in a state of union or *ittehad*, this is the only way to achieve it: through companionship and culture, not through political titles or petitions.

When I hear about instances of Hindu-Muslim enmity, I pray from the depths of my heart for a young person to wake up and give a clarion call for a union of the two communities. Given the current conditions in Sindh, I feel it is the need of the hour that a new young leadership emerges from amongst the Sindhis. Our Sindh has long followed the path of Sufism, and I have faith that it will once again reassert that path over the dissensions that characterise our times. Sindh will become an exemplar for India. May our Sindh take a lead in this union, this *ittehad*.

Preface to the 2nd Edition—*Melaapi Jeevan*

In this new edition, I have added five more chapters. I had written them but did not include them in the first edition that came out in 1941. Hostilities between Hindus and Muslims in Sindh were rife at that time. The formation of Pakistan was being discussed. Hindus had begun to live in fear, with a great sense of foreboding. The publishers advised me that the last five chapters of *Ittehad* would infuriate the Muslims, so it was best to drop them.

Now, after 14 years since that first publication, I believe that Partition divided humanity. The poison of Partition has spread throughout the country. Even Pakistan is divided into two halves, and Allah knows what will happen in the future. This proves that Mr Jinnah's two-nation theory is thoroughly damaging. Truly speaking, humans are bereft of humanity. Greed, avarice, selfishness, and ego were the reasons behind Partition. The urgent need is for Hindus and Muslims to live up to the high ideals of their respective religions and coexist—*ittehad* is needed, *melaapi jeevan* is needed. That can only happen through brotherhood, love, and peace.

No religion teaches hatred and enmity. Therefore, I have named this edition *Melaapi Jeevan*—a harmonious life.

NOTE

The new edition of the book, retitled *Melaapi Jeevan* and the only physical copy available to me, mentions 1983 as the date of reprint. However, Sadarangani specifically mentions 14 years while writing her preface to the new edition, which would make 1955 the publication year of *Melaapi Jeevan*. However, Sadarangani also refers to the 'two halves' of Pakistan, which situates the moment of the new preface after the formation of Bangladesh in 1971. So it is difficult to establish the date of *Melaapi Jeevan* or the new *Ittehad* with certainty. As such, the Sindhi language became part of the Eighth Schedule as a result of the National Policy Resolution passed by Parliament in 1967. The edition that forms the basis of this translation (published in 1983) came about through the government's efforts (through the Ministry of Education and Culture) to enrich and develop materials in the Sindhi language. It is difficult to understand how an edition before this could have been published in India in 1955, considering the Sindhis were scattered all over the country, trying to make ends meet. Given the indifferent archiving and preservation of Sindhi books in India, it is difficult to establish a complete chronology of the publication of this book. It is best to rely on 1983 as the publication year of the revised and reprinted *Ittehad*, which was first published in 1941.

Introduction

I

Dear reader, you hold in your hands a novel by a writer who was hyper-visible in her time but invisible and unknown in ours. Strange and paradoxical though it may seem, Guli Sadarangani's subsequent invisibility is not entirely separate from the negative attention she received during her time. Guli Sadarangani (1906–1994) was the first woman writer of Sindh. However, it is not this uniqueness that made her hyper-visible, nor is there a sufficient celebration of this pioneering achievement. Sadarangani had dared to write a novel about a Hindu-Muslim romance, culminating in marriage. The novel in question was titled *Ittehad* when it first appeared in undivided India in 1941 but was republished and expanded as *Melaapi Jeevan* in 1983 in independent India.

The 1941 version of the novel carried the story of Asha and Hamid, an idealistic couple committed to creating a new secular India. It was originally meant to include another couple (albeit less central to the story) named Zarina and Ranjit, who also marry each other. The second couple involved a Muslim woman and a Hindu man, and according to Sadarangani's publishers, this would infuriate the Muslims. In her words, she was told, 'Musulmaan chhita thee venda.' The last five chapters were dropped from *Ittehad*. However, Sadarangani must have faced ire from her Hindu community also for propagating a marriage between Asha and Hamid. Such was the momentum of opposition and coverage in the newspapers of Karachi and Hyderabad against *Ittehad* that in the future, no mention of the novel would be made without the word 'controversial'.

Sindhi literary histories do not include a full-length study of Sadarangani. In my off-the-record conversations with Sindhi intellectuals, I have sensed sheer dismissal. Almost every entry on Sadarangani in Sindhi literary histories is limited to three or four sentences, as though more was not necessary for this pioneering and courageous writer of her nation. Sadarangani reinserted the missing chapters in a new edition (the basis of this translation) and called it *Melaapi Jeevan*. The shift from an Arabic title to a more Indo-Aryan title could have been strategic. The second edition was released in India, where the Sindhi language was straining to find its place as an Indian language, in script and spirit. However, there is no indication of the reception or rejection of *Melaapi Jeevan*. It does find a mention in a survey from 1984:

> The novel showing Hindu-Muslim marriages aims at propagating various socio-political ideals in society in undivided India, such as Hindu-Muslim unity, inter-caste and inter-provincial marriages, communal harmony, cooperative efforts in industrial and economic fields, encouragement to trade and labour unions and uplift of the downtrodden. It upholds universal brotherhood and shows that the essence of religion lies in the respect shown to other faiths and love for mankind (Jetley, 1984).

The silence this time was not only ideological. The community was struggling to find its footing in a new country, having been rendered asunder and dispersed by Partition. Post-Partition, Sindhi literature has remained restricted to a small group of people who can read and write in Sindhi. Even today, there are fewer readers than writers in Sindhi.

Meanwhile, Sadarangani remains absent from all archives, including those of women writers in India. This specific ignorance about her in Indian literature and her absence from women's archives in India is structural in nature. The region, literature, people, and language of Sindh remain unknown to India even today. Occasionally, other women writers like Popati Hiranandani and Sundri Uttamchandani have been included. They would likely have been recommended by literary experts from the community. It would be a fair speculation to make that these choices were mediated by 'representatives' from the community who did not consider Guli Sadarangani's courageous and historically significant first novel by the first woman writer of Sindh 'safe' for inclusion. There is another structural context to the ignorance surrounding Sindhi literature in general. Save for a few stereotypes, Sindhis remain an unknown and incomprehensible entity for most Indians. I continue to be asked whether Sindhi is a language, if it has literature, or even if Sindhiness is a religion or culture. These questions emerge when there is a sliver of interest in the community; for the most part, I encounter a studied silence. Guli Sadarangani, therefore, belonged to a linguistic and geographical formation that has remained largely unknown, so she is naturally invisible. This first attempt to bring her into the English language is as much an attempt at recovery as it is one of discovery.

II

Sadarangani belonged to a well-heeled, educated class of the Amil group among the Sindhi Hindus. Unusually for her time, Guli Kripalani had a 'love marriage' with Ramchandani Naraindas Sadarangani, a lawyer and freedom fighter. Like the Kayasths of Uttar Pradesh or the Nagars of Gujarat, the Amils have had a long-standing tradition of education and reform. Some of the Amils of Karachi and Hyderabad were as westernised as the Parsis of Bombay. In her study of the community, Saaz Aggarwal (2019) provides various accounts that demonstrate the community's first encounter with modernity. Institutions such as the Brahmo Samaj, brought into Sindh through the Amil community, helped promote women's education and gender-related reform in the region. As a non-Amil Sindhi who came from a family of moneylenders (historically) and shopkeepers, I remember the admiration with which my siblings and I looked up to those we knew as 'Hyderabadi Amils'. To us, they represented the finest and most sophisticated way of being Sindhis: fashionable, somewhat westernised, and most definitely, well-educated. For our purposes, it is important to know that Guli Sadarangani (formerly Kripalani) belonged to a socially privileged caste and class, and the liberalism that characterises *Ittehad* is tied to the emancipatory goals that the Amils attached to education. Although Guli Sadarangani does not explicitly mention their community or caste affiliations, her conception of modern education is quite clear in the way Hamid is a professor of literature. A fair amount of discussion in *Ittehad* is on the importance of education and its role in liberating the lower castes and women from the shackles of oppression.

Sadarangani was a product of numerous historical influences: the modernity of the Amils, a combination of education at Tagore's Shantiniketan and Karachi's prestigious D.J. Sindh College, and the high tide of nationalism. The influence of Shantiniketan must have been profound. In *Ittehad*, the female protagonist, Asha, also studies at Shantiniketan. In fact, Sadarangani (nee Kripalani) was the sister of Krishna Kripalani, a renowned teacher at Shantiniketan who translated Tagore's *Gora* into English (Ganguly, 2022). A recent history of Shantiniketan mentions him but leaves out his sister. It is quite common to find among Sindhi writers a greater commitment to talk of Krishna Kripalani rather than his sister or to make Sadarangani's importance contingent upon the prestige of the family rather than her own achievements. One of the female characters in the novel, Aruna, is a Bengali and a follower of the Brahmo Samaj. This is also a historical phenomenon in Sindh—its close intimacy with the Brahmo Samaj. The male characters are heavily influenced by Gandhi and Nehru. Thus, a period of 60–70 years collapses to form the ideological currents that underlie the novel, making this an important work in the study of the region.

Guli Sadarangani translated Tagore's *Gora* from its English translation into Sindhi. She also translated Nehru's letters to his daughter. The craft of translation led Sadarangani to experiment with writing, and she went on to write several novels, of which *Ittehad* was the first. The narrative flow of the novel reflects the writer's early experience with a new form. However, it is quite remarkable that despite the lack of precedence and experience, Sadarangani chose to write about the seething political questions. Her preoccupation with Tagore's fiction may have played a fairly important role in shaping how she saw her role as a writer. *Ittehad* is set in the decade of the 1940s—a decade characterised by intense anti-colonial churning and shape-shifting political formations. Sindh, in particular, was drawn into the Pakistan movement and became its first site for new experimentation. This period was also the decade that witnessed the strengthening of both Hindu nationalist organisations as well as the Muslim League. Sadarangani's novel reflects the Sufi context of Sindh, as well as emerging fault lines. The developments in Sindh, from the late nineteenth century to the first three decades of the twentieth century, surface in conversations, polemical positions, and anecdotes throughout the novel. The reform movements of the nineteenth century; the tensions between Hindus and Muslims over the demand of Sindh's separation from the Bombay Presidency; and the increasing distrust when electoral arrangements were made along community lines after the Government of India Act in 1935, all this remains a pertinent background to the writing of *Ittehad*. Sadarangani's desire to rescue Sindh from the cesspool of inter-religious differences led her to conceptualise love and equality between religions as both a political and social strategy.

Sadarangani's conception of love between two different religions was not outside Sindh's history and imagination. Studies on Sindh reveal how the Hindus of the region practised non-textual Hinduism, and their intimacy with Sikhism and Sufism set them apart from mainstream Hindus elsewhere in India. While much of what came to be seen as syncretism in Sindh may have been exaggerated in previous accounts (including my previous work), it is an undeniable truth that pirs and shrines were an important part of the lives of Sindhi Hindus. It was not uncommon to see a permeability of what we now define as 'Muslim' culture in the lives of Hindus. This also explains, as I have argued elsewhere (2009), why post-Partition Sindhi Hindus were rejected by upper-caste communities in India, who regarded the Sindhis as impure and too 'Muslim-like'. That being said, the institution of marriage strikes at the heart of caste and religious purity, and Sadarangani's contemporaries found that too extreme a suggestion.

REFERENCES

Aggarwal, Saaz (2019), *The Amils of Sindh: A Narrative History of a Remarkable Community*, Pune: Black-and-White Fountain.

Kothari, Rita (2009, 2nd edition), *The Burden of Refuge: Partition Experience of the Sindhis of Gujarat*, Orient Blackswan.

Ganguly, Swati (2022), *Tagore's University: A History of Visva-Bharati 1921–1961*, Permanent Black.

Jetley, M.K. (November–December 1984), 'The Sindhi Scene: Wanted: More Novels and Plays', *Indian Literature*, Vol. 27, No. 6 (104), pp. 145–153, Sahitya Akademi.

Part I

1

Even as a little girl, Asha demonstrated an artistic bent of mind. She drew alluring and beautiful pictures that left many accomplished artists astonished. She had not been tutored in the formal art of drawing and painting; it was an innate talent. In fact, she had never set foot in a school. Not only could Asha draw and paint, but she could also compose verses. She sang with such melody and heartrending sweetness that her voice provided salve to a wounded heart. Nature had sown many kinds of seeds in Asha, but those seeds had not received the water they needed to blossom. Asha was suffused with many desires and aspirations, but the outlets of expression were few, rather closed. She had to simply rein in her desires.

Asha's parents were narrow-minded and dogmatic about religious practices. They believed that the rules and regulations decreed by custom were not to be changed. They worshipped the entire pantheon of Hindu gods and had contempt for scientific thought. They considered English education dangerous and taught Asha only the Hindi *Ramayana* at home. But nature has its own laws. Asha had quietly eked out her own learning. She was different from the rest—very much her own person. No other advice or legislation got through to her, except the rules of nature in their broadest form. However, out of fear or respect, she did not outwardly show any disagreement with her parents, but she certainly did not accept their instructions in her mind. Only she knew her own secrets. She was a polite and compassionate person but full of courage and quiet sovereignty. While she did not argue publicly, she also did not concede to anything. Wise and patient, she knew that to expect acceptance of her difference was to expect rain in a desert. Those who have patience do not waste their arrows in vain—this was her conviction. A silent Asha's smile showed that someday she would find the freedom to fly away from the cage. 'Don't lose heart, Allah is there for you. The miseries of a hundred years will be taken away in a wink.' She would remember these words by a Sufi poet and feel hopeful. Asha waited for a loving stranger to come into her life. Her eyes were filled with longing as they searched for a beloved amidst deep forests.

Asha's father was a renowned landowner with large tracts of land in the region of Almora. Shankarlal was both stubborn and staunch. He was obsequious towards those in power and oppressed those beneath him. He was generous to those loyal and obedient to him, but he made sure to demolish those who espoused justice and truth, and confronted him. Asha's mother, Gauri Devi, was an innocent and obedient woman but lost in the world of rituals and superstitions. She was extremely pious and did not let anyone needy leave her home empty-handed. She would wake up in the mornings and offer oblations to the sun, the cow, the tulsi plant and then to the home and her husband. In short, she was a compulsive worshipper. If her husband called the day night, or the sun moon, she obediently agreed, with her head lowered. Gauri Devi had no interest beyond her puja and worship. She held the rosary beads all day, constantly muttering away. As luck would have it, she had not been able to bear a son. After much longing, she had managed to give birth to a pretty girl. Gauri Devi loved her daughter dearly. Her daughter's beautiful face filled her with warmth and affection. She believed that by marrying her daughter off, she would find a son in her son-in-law. Meanwhile, Gauri Devi realised that a chasm had formed between Asha and her father. Any suitor suggested by her father was immediately rejected by Asha, who would not even bother to learn more about him. In truth, Asha did not reject the idea of marriage itself. Rather, she waited to fall in love. But where was the lover?

Day and night, Gauri Devi held out her *pallu* before God, pleading for Asha to be blessed with a man she desired—a *dil-guryo* husband, 'one desired by the heart'.

The words *dil-guryo* would fall on Asha's ears, and she hoped that her simple mother's words would bear fruit. Asha was intimidated by her father, but she was protective of her mother, with whom she sympathised. Shankarlal was also very attached to his daughter, but how could Asha's tender heart cope with such intimidating love? Even shackles made of gold imprison. Asha's family had given birth to her body, but her spirit was hunted like prey by a relentless hunter. She felt lonely and solitary, longing for companionship of the heart. There was only one person in the family she could confide in—her cousin, Vijay Kumar.

Vijay's parents passed away when he was just a child. He grew up in his masi's home in Lucknow. His father left him two bungalows and substantial cash, so he never had to depend on anyone for his financial needs. He also did not grow up with the pressure of an elder watching over him; he was free to form his own views on life—unshackled by anyone's expectations except his own. During his school days, Vijay was extremely reckless. Teasing his classmates and teachers was all that school meant to him. His relationship with books was tenuous, rather non-existent. He spent his days frisking and frolicking without a care. But suddenly, there was a change in his life. Through happenstance, he heard a speech by Mahatma Gandhi one day, and it transformed his life. He made a promise to himself that in his adulthood, he would join Gandhi's campaigns and become his ardent follower. That was the beginning of his worshipful relationship with the Mahatma. At the age of 32, Vijay became an active participant in the Congress movement. He worked towards Hindu-Muslim unity and the upliftment of the Harijans. He was the only person Asha considered her confidant and friend. Vijay, in turn, would try to understand Asha's unspoken emotions, eager to know her thoughts better. But unfortunately, Shankarlal did not appreciate the closeness between his nephew and Asha. He almost hated Vijay and considered him an enemy.

As such, Asha and Vijay made use of every opportunity to meet. Vijay would familiarise Asha with the current political situation in the country. He would recite nationalist poetry, filled with the fervour of bravery and resistance. Asha would listen to the uplifting stories her brother told her, often sighing with wistfulness. At times like these, when she felt stirred to act, she had to suppress her excitement and retreat. Vijay was pained to see such a person of truth and beauty reduced to inaction. Her quiet and invisible suffering bothered him, but what could he possibly do? She was unapproachable. In truth, Asha did not confide in him, nor did she seek him out for sympathy. What was the poor man to do?

2

Like a bulbul, Asha would sit under the canopy of trees next to the waterfall and spend days and nights gazing at the blue sky, as if it would part for her and unravel a secret she had been waiting for. She did not trust anyone else with her secret except the tall sky-kissing trees. One day, Asha was so immersed in singing melodious and soul-stirring songs that she was completely oblivious to the world around her. She sensed a hint of a shadow hovering overhead and looked up with a start. It was embarrassing. Vijay stood there with a handsome man. Asha looked at him wide-eyed for a moment, but in the next instant, she lowered her gaze bashfully.

'Asha, this is my Sindhi friend.' Vijay gazed steadily at Asha's face and smiled.

'The one I have heard you praise so many times, right?' Asha asked in a sweet voice, a meaningful and gentle smile playing on her lips.

‘Yes, the one and only: Hamid. We consider the country of Sindh arid and desolate, but the flower that has risen from such a deserted land is far more beautiful than those we find in our temperate climes.’ Vijay looked indulgently at Hamid as he spoke.

An embarrassed Hamid said, ‘Vijay, you haven’t given up your old habit of teasing others, have you? Habits from school days, it seems!’

‘Not at all. I am not teasing, but merely presenting facts. It is for others to see how truthful I am.’

Hamid and Asha gazed into each other’s eyes. Asha’s eyes confirmed the truth of Vijay’s words, and Hamid’s eyes lit up behind his spectacles. Their eyes had managed to convey so much to each other. It was enough. *Ruh ka rihaan*, the souls had conversed.

3

Vijay and Hamid had not only studied together at the same school but also attended the same college. Vijay passed his law examination, while Hamid completed his Master's degree and left for Europe. Vijay had barely practised law when Mahatma Gandhi initiated the Satyagraha movement. Who could have stopped the storm raging inside a young mind? With abandon, Vijay set aside his education and career and jumped into the flames to make a sacrifice. He did not pause to ask himself if there was any fear or ponder the consequences. He had to follow the footsteps of the Mahatma—that was it. Vijay was arrested and spent some time in jail. When he was released, the movement had subsided. He no longer felt like going back to his legal profession. Meanwhile, the Congress had founded a new periodical, *Azaad Hindustan*, which began being published from Allahabad. Vijay was appointed its editor.

Hamid was awarded a Doctor of Literature in London. Armed with his new degree, he returned to India. The college in Lucknow where he had been a student now invited him to join as a professor. Hamid was a gentle and low-key person, yet he had a big heart and a sharp mind. His refined and delicate manners, handsome face, and pleasing speech left people enthralled. It was evident from the early days of his childhood that he had the makings of a great poet. As he grew older, Hamid acquired more fluency in several languages and spoke English, Gujarati, and Bengali like a native. He was also deeply immersed in *Shah Jo Risalo*, Tagore's writings, and Shelley's poetry. When Hamid looked at people, he did not look upon them as Hindus or Muslims. They were extensions of a large universe in which caste, religion, and sectarianism did not matter. For him, they were *Khalik jee khalqa*, the creations of the Lord, to be judged and recognised by their actions and principles. Hamid had also familiarised himself with the tenets of numerous religious philosophies and could see how many branches stemmed from the same tree. In fact, he had long ceased to identify himself by sect or religion.

Hamid came from a highly respected family in Sindh. His father, Umed Ali, was a senior government officer and the first Sindhi Muslim to become a collector. A just and kind man, Umed Ali was neither deeply religious nor allured by bribery. He preferred to spend his life as a God-fearing and God-loving man. His begum, Roshan

Ara, was from a renowned family in Uttar Pradesh. Like many women of her time, she was also at the forefront of social reforms, rejecting purdah and seeking refuge in education. A beautiful and sophisticated woman, Roshan Ara approached people with kindness and confidence. In that sense, Hamid was very much like his mother, although his sense of justice was perhaps a trait he inherited from his father. Roshan Ara had sent Hamid to her natal home in Lucknow so that he could receive a better education.

Hamid had spent most of his adolescent and youthful years away from Sindh. Yet, he had a love for Sindh. He felt a longing for it. He would grow restless to return to his *watan*. While passing through the wilderness of Sindh, he found himself looking for the immortal pair of Sasui and Punhun from Shah Abdul Latif's *Risalo*. Similarly, the story of Umar and Marvi, narrated by Shah, would come rushing back to his mind. He felt Shah was a living presence in Sindh.

Yet, Hamid also felt like an outsider. Sindh was a stifling place for someone with a literary sensibility. Its people were busy emulating the ways of the West, and beyond concerns of earning money and following fashion, they had scant appreciation for anything literary or cultural. The bankruptcy of culture pained Hamid. How could this slumber be broken and this slavishness removed? He had a right—or perhaps a duty—to do more for his native land. But it was Uttar Pradesh that had nurtured him, shaping his political and literary tastes and helping him become the cosmopolitan person he was.

Hamid would spend a few days with family and relatives, but then he would spend the rest of his vacation in the embrace of nature, heading to a mountainous region. What else is a poet to do if not stay close to nature? What else would offer him solace and inspiration if not nature? Even this time during his vacation, nature beckoned him. Perhaps some karmic force attracted him to a primal relation, a friend in the hills. And so, Hamid found himself in Almora. On seeing him approach, Vijay's joy knew no bounds. He had been urging his beloved friend to visit Almora, but Hamid kept putting off the plan. Hamid rushed to embrace his friend and said, 'Vijay, it was your affection and my longing that could not stop me from coming this time. So, here I am!'

'*Arre dost*, since when does the flower bother about the bulbul, or the moon about the chakor bird, or the flame wait for the moth?' Vijay smiled and replied.

'Alright, make what you will of my decision to come! But first, tell me, where's my dear sister-in-law, Aruna bhabhi?'

'She's visiting a friend and should be here any moment. In the meantime, freshen up and have some tea. You must be tired.'

'No, no, my bhabhi will give me tea. I won't enjoy it otherwise. There she is!'

On unexpectedly seeing Hamid at her home, Aruna Devi squealed with joy. '*Arre*, how did this brother of mine suddenly emerge?'

'Behan, a brother is always there for his sister,' Hamid replied with affection. 'But bhabhi, tell me how did you manage to make friends in the hills? People in these regions are so rigid and illiterate in their ways. Surely, you must have found someone who can please you. Have you found such a friend?'

Aruna quipped, 'If the jungles of Sindh can produce a flower like you, how can the beauty of this region not produce so much more?'

Hamid was embarrassed and immediately conceded, 'Granted, you have defeated me. You always leave me speechless. You know I have been carrying a dream since childhood: I want to see a woman like this in India—one who is an active participant and an equal to men. You inspire me with such confidence. You will make my dream come true.'

'Oh, I am nothing! You should see my friend, Asha. She's the kind of woman who will make your dream seem real. A picture of both physical and inner beauty, she will bring happiness and prosperity to any home—a testament to the spiritual maturity of an Indian woman. The more I look at her, the more I realise that there's so much more to her than what she expresses. Every day, a new layer of beauty reveals itself.' Aruna spoke with excitement.

'I feel that there's much about her that eludes me. Despite our close interactions, I will never truly get to know her fully,' Vijay added wistfully.

Hamid could not wait to meet such a woman, but he felt inhibited to express his wish, so he changed the subject.

'Alright, alright, have you forgotten my tea, bhabhi? You seem lost in praising your friend,' Hamid teased.

'Come on, bhai! How could I forget you? Are you any less important than Asha? Here comes your tea!'

Hamid smiled sheepishly.

4

The sky remained overcast. The clouds from the previous night had not stopped thundering, and it had taken ages for the rain to cease. Lightning flashed every now and then. Hamid had been introduced to Asha that morning. At night, he was a restless soul. An inexplicable pain poked at his heart. He tried hard to soothe it under the new ashy dawn, but his heart continued to echo the thunderous clouds. He wanted to shed tears to lighten this heaviness, but no tears came. What kind of state is this? Is this what nature intended? Is that why I was brought to Almora? Ya Allah, what have you done to me? Is that how helpless *ishq* renders humans? What does this mischief by nature mean? These *qissas* belong to the realm of poetic dreams. Why should I be shackled by them? This is a difficult journey. Why should I undertake it? The heart and the head wrestled with each other. Hamid tried to sleep, to drift away, but in vain. He felt engulfed by fear. Just as leaves and twigs are helpless, simply conceding to the breeze, human beings are affected by their *kismet*. A numb and fearful Hamid lay in bed, invaded by an army of sensations.

In the morning, Hamid sat up and took a few sips of water. He knew that something mysterious had happened to him. His body was experiencing new sensations, and old meanings had become uncertain. He allowed all this to wash over him and walked around in a trance. He came to a halt when the heartbreakingly sweet words of a ghazal reached his ears. Startled, he turned around, and his eyes fell upon an image of beauty, who was engrossed in singing. 'Ah, Nature! What kind of coincidence is this? I seem to have come to the same waterfall as Asha... Asha, are you truly the hope of my life?' Asha was busy humming and walking. Upon seeing Hamid before her, she blushed. This was the first time in her life that she was looking at a man without anyone else present. She had never been allowed to go out to study or mingle with others. But Asha smiled and greeted him comfortably. Even though it took courage, she seemed confident. A reassured Hamid asked, 'Do you come every day to this waterfall?'

'Yes, I have a deep friendship with this waterfall.' Asha smiled.

'The waterfall is indeed fortunate. But I wonder if it knows how fortunate it is.'

'People learn from books, but how am I to learn? I have not had the fortune to read books. Nature, and this waterfall in particular, is my book. It is my window to the universe. I am grateful to this university of nature, my confidant,' Asha added.

'Absolutely, you are fortunate to have been born amidst such natural beauty. Our Sindh is a dry and arid land.'

'Wilderness has its own beauty. Perhaps we are limited in our ability to appreciate it. Surely, forests also conceal mysteries that we mortals are unable to unravel.'

'That makes sense, and it also explains how the poets of Sindh composed verses upon witnessing the aridity of the land. But we lack the eye and the soul to see that beauty.'

'My eyes have become so satiated by these tall, verdant trees that I now long to see open fields!' Asha said.

'Understandably, we long for what is not available to us. The streams of desire continue to flow, aching to reach places they have never been. I suppose this is what characterises life—this restlessness—and perhaps it is an exercise in living.'

'Living is also about resting and not only exercising,' Asha replied.

Hamid sighed, reminded of the tumultuous night he had spent. He realised how he longed for a reprieve. This restlessness must stop. Perhaps it was better to stay away from Asha. As a way of bidding her farewell, he muttered, 'Vijay must be looking for me. I didn't even tell him I was going for a walk. I just wandered off. Aruna bhabhi must also be waiting for me to join them for breakfast. I better go, or they'll think I'm lost.'

'*Theek hai.* You should return now. Vijay dada's house is not very far from here.'

'Do you often visit Vijay's house?'

'Occasionally. Not that often. If someone's ill...' Asha hesitated.

Hamid was tempted to ask more, but he was much too civilised to probe further. They bid each other goodbye by exchanging a glance. Asha left for home, while Hamid stood rooted to the spot. Once she disappeared into the thick shade of the trees and was out of view, he took a few steps, almost in a trance. He was startled by the sound of Aruna's laughter.

'*Wah bhai wah*, there you are, brother! You keep running, and we keep chasing you,' Aruna teased him.

'Let him be! Nature exacts its own revenge. Someday, he may have to come chasing us!' Vijay joined Aruna in teasing Hamid.

'Friend, forget about this debate. It's hardly my fault if I get disoriented in a foreign land. I was, in fact, anxious to find you and knew that you would find me even if I didn't,' Hamid said with a smile.

'But do you know? In the process of looking for you, I lost my friend. I usually meet her here, but today it seems as if she has already gone or not appeared. Thank God, I found you in the same place,' Aruna remarked.

Hamid became serious. 'She did come here, but she left quickly. Perhaps I intimidated her. We men tend to forget that women feel embarrassed by unwanted attention. I should have been more sensitive.'

'The truth is, my friend, Asha, is shy, but you are also so shy and inhibited. Do you remember when we first met? I had to make all the overtures and keep the conversation going. Vijay kept goading me, asking me to talk to you and mingle with you. I was a bit resentful. I mean, as a woman, why should I be the one making the effort to initiate a friendship?'

Hamid threw his head back and laughed. 'That's very convenient! Why hanker after equality with men then? If you want the rights men enjoy, you should be ready to give up these feminine inhibitions. You don't want to give that up either, do you?'

'Oh, come on! If women give up their womanhood, what beauty is left then?' Aruna retorted.

'Then why the desire to mimic us? Why do you intrude upon our realm? Stay within your own sphere, and leave ours to us.'

'If you think we are mimicking you men, you are mistaken. We seek not to copy but to claim our rights as human beings. Women seek justice. Indian men don't want to do justice to women. They think women are as good as zero, with no value of their own. Women are living beings; they have their own strength and desires. Indian men do not want women to have any strength or any value. Look at the social injustice: women are under men's oppression. All rules apply only to women. Religion was invented to keep women in control and so were laws. Men are free to do as they please. Should no rules apply to them?'

'So you must prefer the social structures of advanced nations.' Hamid laughed.

'Undoubtedly, I prefer the social structures of the West. There is no injustice to women there. Women have equal rights and equal opportunities. They have not been made into inferior people,' Aruna replied.

'So you consider the West to be more civilised and progressive, right?' Hamid asked.

'That may or may not be true. At the heart of Western civilisation lies a void. The West lacks high ideals or moral principles to aspire to. Social arrangements are a product of historical circumstances. In the West, the conditions for liberty are not created through a sense of social and spiritual collectivism. Materialistic and scientific progress stands in danger of fragmentation and dissension because without a spiritual foundation, it will not be able to sustain itself. It carries the seeds of greed and selfishness. A one-sided progress will not take us very far. We should not blindly imitate the West. We may end up adopting its flaws and slide into an abyss. We will also be drawn into a materialistic vortex. I believe that, now that our nation is in the midst of flux, we are beginning to develop some awareness. We must tread carefully and not ape the West, lest we lose our own way,' Vijay said with farsightedness.

'No, no, Vijay, we are not going to slide into an abyss. Our country is not going to lose its ancient culture. Sometimes, clouds may eclipse the sun, but that does not mean there will be darkness forever. Our civilisation cannot remain hidden behind the eclipse for long. The sun will always rise from the East and spread its light even to the West. This sun will shine again. I am confident. Slavery has made us weak and helpless, but our self-respect and spirit of independence have been ignited. There will come a time when we will speak of our *mulk*, our country, with pride,' Aruna spoke with fervour.

'Absolutely, we should not lose hope at this stage. In fact, the star of hope shines brightly over India now. Our leader, Mahatma Gandhi, is the avatar of independence. He holds the reins of our *kismet*, and it is he who will rescue us from self-doubt and reestablish *Ram rajya* for us,' Vijay added with conviction.

'*Dost*, with all due respect, I have a different opinion on this matter. I do not believe that the future of India should rely upon an idealised version of the past. This is like trying to awaken the dead. Nature's law dictates that what lives today must die tomorrow. When we cast a historical gaze upon time, we can see that every age produced its own messiah. While it is true that the teachings of all messiahs may lead us to the same place, every messiah is special to their age. The circumstances of each era are different, and for that reason, every leader, every messiah has had to invent their own strategies and methods unique to that age. It's one thing to derive pride from the past, to even learn from its lessons, but we cannot become nostalgic about it and want our present to be shaped by its shadow. That would be a derivate present, and I believe that the real is always superior to a copy,' Hamid said nonchalantly.

'Hamid bhai, I am in complete agreement with you,' Aruna supported him joyfully. 'Indian men, no matter how free or open to changes from all parts of the world, will still insist on women's chastity.'

'Yes, my sister, you are right. We men have been victims of egotism. Women manage to kill their egotism. A woman uses the dagger of love and cuts through all the flab that forms an egoistic demeanour.'

'But men also claim to be in love,' Aruna quipped.

'So what if they do? What is true love for a man? Where is his willingness to sacrifice? Women are much more accomplished in this arena. If women try to be like men in this respect, they will bring themselves down from the sky to the earth,' Hamid said.

'But are there men deserving of the kind of love women give to them? They exploit her love and selflessness and turn her into an object, a toy. They find ways and means to annihilate her very sense of self,' Aruna responded.

'Because men feel insecure by the growing brilliance of women; they fear it will dim their own light. A man can only flourish and feel secure by undermining her,' Hamid continued.

'So what you are saying is that fundamentally, men are more selfish than women,' Aruna said.

'Of course, this is man's weakness. It is his prison—this masculine self. Women can soften the edges of this egotism. Women's strength lies in love and their dynamism, not in their obstinate stance. Women can diffuse male obstinacy by being strategic. One ego cannot diffuse another ego,' Hamid added.

Vijay laughed and said to Aruna, 'Did you hear that? One ego cannot diffuse another. You also learn to deal with my egotism and pacify it.'

'No, no, I am not saying that women have to be subservient to men, and that's how they deal with their egotism. They must maintain their own sense of self. I am only emphasising the role of love and persuasion. It will permeate through the dense walls of masculinity. Of course, there may be those who remain completely untouched and will, in fact, take advantage of women's love and sacrifice.'

'This means that men will continue to do this to women,' Aruna added angrily.

'It's basically women's dependence on men that allows them to do that. That's true. Women should also have the right to divorce and remarry.'

'But what is most crucial is that from childhood, girls should be encouraged to study and receive training so that they are confident. They should be equipped to navigate life without men, earn and support themselves, rather than remain helpless. In fact, empowered women can show men how strong they are and shine in their own field or sphere. In my view, Indian women have shortchanged themselves, and that is why the Indian man has become the monster he is today.' Hamid spoke with passion.

'I understand women are also responsible for their fate. If the oppressed do not recognise oppression, where is the starting point for change?' Aruna said.

'Alright, three cheers for women!' Vijay laughed and concluded.

5

Shankarlal rested his back against a wall and sat down, his expression grave. He looked at this daughter with concern. 'My child, be good. Stop being childish. Don't torture an old man like me. It's been two years since I have been banging my head against the wall. You refuse to listen to anyone. Why don't you tell me what's going on? Please confide in me. I just can't understand the reason behind your silence. Normally, elders interpret girls' silence as a sign of shyness. But your silence is cold and heartless, sheer stubbornness. Foolish that I am, I have been waiting for your consent. Ordinarily, there is no practice of seeking a child's consent. Parents decide matrimonial issues and get their daughters married. People in the community are already gossiping. I feel so ashamed some days and wish for the Earth to open up and swallow me. My own daughter refuses to obey me. I have to carry all this weight and embarrassment alone. How unlucky I am to have no son! After many prayers and longing, I was blessed with a daughter. I thought a son-in-law would be like a son to me, but even that is not to be. And look at your mother, she is hardly of any help to me. She goes around muttering mantras all day. Men feel at ease when their wives have some sense.

Putta, who is to tell how long I will live. Death may happen any day—if not today, perhaps tomorrow. I have collected much wealth and have worked so hard for it. Whom do I leave this to? I wish that bloody Vijay had never been born. Anyway, think about this, putta, I will die, leaving you and your mother helpless. Listen to me, child. Obey your father and see how happy you become. Boys like Vinod Kumar are not easy to find. He has just finished his engineering from Pune. I have heard he has been offered a good job in Punjab. The boy has no vices; he is such an *ashraf* and a religious person. He neither smokes nor drinks. Nor does he eat meat. I have also secretly learnt that he is keen to marry a beautiful woman. I can aim an arrow here quite successfully. Tell me, child, tell me. Let me know today.'

'Father, I am so sorry I have disappointed you. I have not been able to fulfil your wishes and aspirations.' Asha spoke with trepidation.

'Does your heart not break to do this to me? I need to know the reason.' Shankarlal spoke gently.

'I find it heartbreaking. It bothers me day and night.'

'So why don't you listen to me? What is stopping you? Why do you sound helpless?'

'My heart does not listen to me. The very thought of marriage makes me shudder.'

'Does it even make sense to feel fear before the act has been committed?'

'But this fear is natural for young women before they marry. There's nothing unusual about it. The truth is, I'm not afraid of the prospect of another person. It is my own heart that scares me,' Asha explained.

'Putta, once you are married, you will feel better.'

'But what if I don't feel better? Would that not be an injustice to me and to someone else? I may be guilty of disobedience, but I cannot say yes to this.'

Shankarlal bellowed, 'I think someone has destroyed your senses. So, what is your heart saying? And do all the girls who marry not have hearts? What is the hesitation?'

'I know only about myself.'

'So, like Western girls, you also want to romance with someone before marriage? Have you turned this *adharmi*, this irreligious? All this is the result of that wretched Vijay. Rascal! He didn't bother looking at the girls in our own caste and went ahead and married a loose Brahmo Bengali woman. That Gandhi maharaj has led everyone astray. He's at the root of this chaos. All the young men now think they can wear khadi and go to jail, and that's all they need to do. Now they want the untouchables and the Hindus to mix. They want to take away wealth from the wealthy. Ask them how differences and hierarchies will disappear from this vast universe. Some are born high, and some are born low because it is their karma that makes them so. Gandhi's latest tune is that Hindu and Muslim unity will ensure *swaraj*. Really, it is the beginning of Kaliyug, ever since this bloody Mahatma has become important. And now, listen to that audacious and communist woman, Aruna! She says only once caste and communal differences go away will India become free. I saw her with a Muslim man yesterday with my own eyes. Shame on a husband who gives such freedom to his wife! I have heard that he lives in her house.

Beware, Asha, if you step foot into that house! I can't stand that shameless girl. She goes everywhere with her husband. She fraternises with the low castes, Muslims, cultivators, and all kinds of people. But she is never to be found in a temple. I feel like calling a panchayat meeting and getting both of them ostracised from the community. But they will turn around and shamelessly say they couldn't be bothered about the panchayat.'

Shankarlal stormed out of the room.

Asha sat still, shivering with fear. She had barely spoken a few words and had already heard such awful things about her friends. Religious differences had made the world such an unhappy place. Her father had reminded her today that she was a Hindu, and Hamid, a Muslim. She had not thought of them that way.

Hum-zaati are people whose souls have met. If God does not use labels, why do we? Would the Hindu God be different from the Muslim God? Not at all. There can only be one, a nameless one. No human being is free from virtues and vices, and that is all there is to it. If a Hindu considers himself superior to others because he thinks he is purer, his actions towards others should reflect that and not involve throwing filth at them or becoming filthy himself. In her pure heart, there was no sense of otherness towards any religion or caste. Her God was beyond all this.

6

When Asha did not see Aruna, she became restless. She desperately wanted to go and find out what had happened. But her father's threatening voice rang in her ears. A shudder ran through her body. What should she do? Asha had tried her best not to disobey her father, but today, some mysterious force pulled her away. She could not stop herself. When the water in a sea is calm, the sea flows within its limits and boundaries. But when, for some reason, the water becomes restless, the sea knows no boundaries. It overflows into foreign territories and floods them. Asha's heart had become like the sea, suddenly transformed into a fierce force. Years of silencing had caused her heart to erupt. How long could it resist the heat of the sun? Her heart was but a small lamp. How long could it hold out? The world can turn you into a coward, but confidence and an irresistible attraction can turn cowards into warriors. That's who Asha had become today.

Since childhood, Asha carried a conviction that love was the most sacred of all. She was a worshipper of love. And love is put through severe tests. The outward appearance of love may be alluring and pleasing, drawing the lover with promises of solace and joy. But love is not easy. Asha knew that. It's a strange *leela*, this love.

Asha stepped into Aruna's house. Her mind was like a battlefield. The servant informed her that Aruna and Vijay were not at home. Her hopes dashed, she despondently turned to leave. A voice reached her ears. She turned around and saw Hamid walking in her direction. The sight of him made her knees go weak, and her heart began to race. Her face flushed crimson, and her body trembled. She could not summon the courage to even smile and say namaste. As for Hamid, his smile was gentle, his eyes tender, and his voice had sensitivity and refinement.

'Vijay and Aruna should be back any moment. You've walked so far, why don't you rest for a bit? You are panting from such a long walk.' Hamid shifted the chair in her direction.

Asha did not know how to refuse her beloved's request. She sat down, her head lowered. But her heart drummed violently, almost audible to Hamid. 'Are you alright? Why are you panting so much?' Hamid's voice was anxious.

Asha raised her head and gazed at him with deer-like eyes. She seemed to have lost her voice. Her eyes had moistened. She almost whispered, 'I am absolutely fine. I probably walked too fast.'

'I hope you have not stayed back out of fear. I hope I have not been too forward. Are these tears from the exhaustion of the body...?' Hamid could speak no further.

'Fear? About what?' Asha wiped her eyes.

Hamid's eyes also moistened. They looked at each other, and time came to a standstill.

Hamid finally broke the silence. 'Asha Devi, seeing you has stirred feelings within me that I find unsettling. I am bewildered by the intensity of these new feelings. It has left me baffled. But I want to assure you that I will not take a single step towards you without your consent. Whatever boundary you draw and place you assign me, I will consider that my limit and remain within it. But I had to express how I feel, at least once. My apologies. I don't have many words to convey the depth of my emotions, but I hope it is acceptable to you.'

Asha could not find her voice. Like a helpless child, she looked into Hamid's eyes. Hamid's heart trembled with fear and joy as he continued, 'Such endeavours are frightening. There are vast chasms between us and to cross them...'

'In the world of love, there are no considerations. The path of love is different from that of the world.' Asha's voice was now calm.

'Your courage makes me feel small. I am weak in comparison. But the rules for women are harsher. I don't want my presence to taint your sacred life or jeopardise your dignity. I just don't have the temerity to do that.' Hamid sighed with sadness.

Asha saw Hamid's defeated expression and smiled. 'But if I am not frightened by social oppression, are you going to make me feel scared? In my view, such obstacles exist to test us. Without these tests, how would we distinguish truth from falsehood?'

'I feel ashamed at seeing your courage and candour. My fears have receded, and I feel emboldened. I only want to say that from today, nothing matters more to me than you. I am the devotee of your love. Do not ever lose faith in me. If we are not able to meet or even see each other, do not forget this. Do not ever doubt me, no matter what happens.' Hamid's eyes sparkled with fire.

'We will find out how truthful your vows are! For now, you need to grant me something to mark this moment.' Asha spoke with bemusement and tenderness.

'Undoubtedly. Just ask!'

'From now on, I will not be *aap* for you. You must use the familiar *tum* instead.'

'Okay, but you must give me the same honour. I hope you will also give me the same privilege.'

'If it's a bargain, sure, I'll keep up my end of the deal,' Asha laughed.

'What's the point of free things? This kind of bargain adds value.'

'What if I don't have the means to pay the value of such priceless things? What if they remain beyond my reach?'

'In that case, it's the gratitude that counts!'

'I will remain grateful to you. I have no way to thank you.'

'We are equal, and please speak to me as an equal. Don't embarrass me again. I don't want your voice to carry the shadow of women's unequal position. We are going to be the new voices of a world where nobody is a slave to another. Both men and women will have claims to the same things: the same respect, the same justice. It will be a world of *ittehad*, of union. Once our country unfurls the flag of independence, it will be a new tomorrow. We must ensure that this happens.'

Asha's face filled with pride and happiness. She said, 'Allow me to go now. Dada and bhabhi have still not returned.' She stood up.

'How can you expect me to let you go? But I will not stop you if you wish to go,' Hamid said in the most tender and heartbreaking voice. Asha left, her eyes smiling with newfound joy.

Hamid sat down, and the world of dreams beckoned him. Had Aruna and Vijay not shown up, he would have remained oblivious to everything around him. But Aruna entered, as she always did, with a loud and cheerful voice. Hamid quickly collected himself and pretended as if nothing had happened.

'Hamid bhai, guess what I've got for you? Come on, make a guess and I'll give it to you!' Hamid had seen the postman at some distance, so he promptly said, 'Love from Sindh?'

'You're absolutely right! Who is it from?' Aruna asked.

'Mother!' Hamid picked up the letter from his mother, which seemed like another sign from the universe. He sought the privacy of his room.

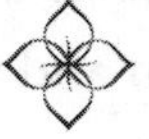

7

Karachi
2 May 1938

Noor-e-chashm, the light of my eyes,

May you remain well, and may Allah keep you healthy and prosperous. I read your letter. It made me happy but also somewhat sad. You have run away to the mountains of Almora. If a mother has waited for months and months to see her son, counting every single day until their meeting, and then the son chooses to be treacherous and run away, would the mother not have enough reason to feel sad and disappointed, tell me? But strange are maternal hearts! So soft and so changeable. One moment, I felt sad, but in the next, I said to myself, 'Never mind. The weather here is very hot. Let him go to the mountains and experience the pleasant air.' Now, you better stay true to your promise and return on the 15th. Your father is aching to meet you. Gulu and Zarina pine for their brother and pester me with questions like, 'When is bhai coming?' But look at you, so heartless, made of marble! What can I even say?

Putta, I need to talk to you about a private matter. I avoided bringing it up all these days. I was looking for a peaceful moment when I could talk to you in person. How could I bring up such a delicate matter in a letter? Ideally, I would have liked to speak in person, but since you have delayed your arrival so much, I have to bring it up. Your father's friend, Khan Bahadur Inayat Ali Khan, has recently been appointed the district judge of Sukkur. He had spent a few days here with us and brought his daughter, Shireen, along. You might remember we met her three years ago when we visited Kashmir and stopped in Amritsar en route. She was pursuing an MA at the time. Now she has earned her degree and even visited Europe with her father. Inayat Ali broached the subject of establishing relations with us, as in, a betrothal between the two of you. We expressed our consent, but I did say that it was important to talk to both the boy and the girl these days. Times have changed. We are waiting to know your thoughts. The girl seemed very willing; the rest is up to you.

Just yesterday Inayat Ali reminded us about his offer again. I hope you will let us know your wish once you receive this letter. And I hope it will be in the affirmative. There's no reason for refusal. The girl is suitable for you in every respect. She can be a little spoilt, but that's inevitable given how much she has been pampered. With a partner like you, she will cease to be impetuous and will settle down.

Your father is overjoyed at the prospect of a daughter-in-law coming into the home. You are also thirty years old, so it's not an untimely suggestion. What else can I write? You are wise beyond your years. May you flourish and remain happy.

Blessings,
Your Amma

Upon reading the letter, Hamid almost felt dizzy. He had been lost in the world of dreams. Suddenly, he was unceremoniously thrown to the ground. The ground had puddles and potholes, pebbles and stones. Oh, the misery of being brought back to reality! How lovely it was to stroll in the paradise of love and desire! He felt engulfed by doubts and misgivings. He could only see enemies around him. 'I had barely enjoyed a few moments of love, and now this disaster. I had tried to escape the clutches of love, but now I am caught in its web,' he said to himself. 'On the other hand, look at Asha—a gentle soul but with such courage. I have to hand it to her. Clearly, men only have physical prowess. They can dominate, but they lack the courage and conviction. There's an onslaught of emotions, but there's little steadiness.' He felt like unburdening himself to his friend, but he would betray someone's else secret, and he didn't have the right to do so. Finally, he sat down to respond to his mother.

Almora
5 May 1938

My dear mother,

Guilty as charged. No wonder I am spoilt. I have such a gracious and forgiving mother in you. You forgive me without giving me a chance to make amends. Seriously, only you could have managed to rein in a fugitive son like me. May Allah give you a long life.

Your letter was a delight to read, and I missed your presence so much. I thought I would bring you some joy by writing back to you immediately. Amma, do you want to send your son away and make him distant from you? You think I have a heart of marble now. Just imagine if it were to turn into iron later! Abba and you have chosen a daughter-in-law for yourselves, but how about giving me a chance to select my wife? Are you seeking my consent on a decision you have already made? No, you are much too just to be unfair to me. Do you think I care about degrees and reputation? Perhaps I once did. But there may be more important things in my life now. I don't have a dearth of intelligent people around me, but I seek a partner who is largehearted, one who can bring grace and spiritual pleasure to my existence. Rest, in person.

My regards to Abba and love to Gulu and Zarina.

I seek your blessings, always.

Your son,
Hamid

8

Hamid had barely finished the letter when Aruna asked him to join her and Vijay for dinner. The moment he sat down at the dinner table, Aruna teased him, '*Arre* Hamid bhai, the letter was really from Amma, wasn't it? The radiance on your face tells a different story.'

'Does my expression look joyful or sad?' Hamid asked.

'That I can't say. But you are secretive today. There's some turmoil inside you,' Aruna said.

'No, behan, Amma's letter is very much on my mind. But you don't think Amma's letter can cause turmoil? It contains some good news.'

'Pray tell!' Vijay quickly added.

'How will I rest without telling you? Amma has chosen a girl for me.'

'*Arre wah!* Such great news! I will have a bhabhi now!' Vijay said.

'And I will acquire a friend!' Aruna chimed in.

'What if you don't like her?' Hamid asked.

'How can your choice not work for us? You have exquisite taste, I am sure,' Aruna said.

'It's not my choice,' Hamid said.

'It must be your choice. Perhaps Amma has a hand in it,' Aruna said confidently.

'You can see that I am here. I don't even know that many Sindhis.'

'If not a Sindhi, she must be from some other community. You must have selected someone.'

'I did not look for anyone, nor do I plan to. You know well that I am a shy person.'

'Such calm waters run deep! You are an *ustaad* hiding behind the veil of shyness,' Aruna declared.

'No, behan, I will be happy if you were to look for someone for me. I am no *ustaad*.'

'What if your mother does not like the one I choose?'

'You can leave that to me,' Hamid said.

'Really? Then let me ask you a question, if you don't mind. I have often wondered what your views are about inter-regional and inter-caste marriages.'

'That's a difficult one,' Hamid paused. 'To tell you the truth, I don't even believe in religious and caste differences—all that *zaati ikhtalafin*. I find such sectarianism or *firqa parasti* a sign of illiteracy. If we can form lifelong friendships across communities, and that is not a problem, then marriage is just a step away. Undoubtedly, it is revolutionary from a social perspective, but it is certainly not a crime. If we view the idea of marriage as a union of souls rather than of castes, I am confident that in the nation of souls, there are no religious and caste differences. Such differences are the result of primitive thinking and narrow minds and hearts. For those who have truly understood the essence of religion, or who are innocent, like children, of such religious differences, these differences do not matter. Not in their imagination. Not in the slightest.'

'But in the worldly theatre, the social perspective reigns over many other viewpoints. We can't ignore that fact,' Aruna said.

'Sure. But marriages can be seen from two perspectives: love and social acceptance. Which of the two matters more depends on individuals. Every person must ask themselves what is more important, weigh both sides and then decide.'

'Inter-regional marriages, of course, involve differences in language and customs. But inter-caste or inter-religious marriages are more difficult to resolve—the question of religion is the toughest,' Vijay said with some doubt.

'Undoubtedly, this is a difficult issue. But the only solution is to expunge the political and public sphere from religious interference. If people bring in religion, it should be considered a civil transgression or even a crime.'

'What do you mean?' Aruna asked.

'This is how it happens: Let me give you examples of small, trivial things that have paved the way for *zaati-nafaq* or *firqah warana ikhtilafat*, communal differences. This poison has taken many forms now. When you travel between Sindh and Punjab, you will hear two distinct calls for water: Hindu water and Muslim water. Hindu roti, Muslim roti. Such voices fan communal differences. Even public places, restaurants, parks, and clubs are separate for Hindus and Muslims. Schools are separate, neighbourhoods are separate. How can differences not multiply? How will Hindus and Muslims coexist? Will enmity and distance not persist if we can't even have common spaces? How will this *ittehad* happen? I believe we need to address these issues at their roots. Otherwise, these differences will only grow wider in the future. If Hindus despise Muslims and practise untouchability, Muslims will condemn Hindus. Such behaviour towards each other only fans sectarianism. Let me give you a recent example. There's a new neighbourhood coming up in Karachi called Jamshed quarter. This is the twentieth century, and yet it is so unfortunate that while we claim to support reform and modern education, we still have colonies named after every religion, even in a city like Karachi. There's a Hindu colony, a Muslim colony, a Parsi colony, and a Christian colony—all separate from each other. It is astonishing that even the Hindu colony is divided into further factions. The Hindus of Sindh are anyway busy pulling each other down.'

'I don't understand how the Karachi Municipality even allowed such a risky arrangement,' Vijay remarked.

'Because the government is interested in creating these factions. How else will it rule, if not by dividing?' Hamid responded.

'But we have to admit that Hindus do have this problem. If they can't unite among themselves, how do we expect them to coexist with Muslims with feelings of brotherhood and affection?' Vijay said with exasperation.

'Of course, these religious and caste issues destroy communities. But what unity exists among Muslims? The Shias and Sunnis fight with each other all the time. Faith is so benign, but look at the dangerous outcomes of religion.' Hamid's voice was filled with despair.

'That's true. But this disease of untouchability has also stemmed from Hinduism. The government has created the Communal Award precisely based on these fissures,' Vijay responded.

'That's why I am saying that in the political realm, religion has no place. Such sectarianism must be declared criminal. Religion must be a private matter, a spiritual pursuit. Religion may have an ethical side to it, but it must remain a personal practice. Religion has a relation with the inner life, and that's where it should belong—in the inner realm. That's it!' Hamid spoke forcefully. 'But these things can be implemented only if we have our own government. A foreign government is only interested in creating divisions. It is not interested in the *ittehad* of Hindus and Muslims. Hindu-Muslim unity will make foreign rule impossible.'

'Of course, these separate electorates are a ploy to increase these distances. The British government is making sure that Hindus and Muslims remain separate and inimical to each other. It is people like us who are foolish. We get instigated so easily,' Vijay added.

'Vijay, this will happen. It's human tendency to have one's own self-interest in mind. Where is human greed to go? When these fires are fanned, this is bound to happen,' Hamid said.

'But are you sure that if we cease to have a foreign government, we will coexist peacefully? I feel the cultural and theological differences between Hindus and Muslims are so vast that it is unlikely they will be able to live with each other's differences,' Aruna intervened.

'You are right. But tell me, what differences exist between us? Do we not coexist?' Hamid replied to Aruna.

'That's because our foundation is the same. We have eradicated ignorance by keeping our eyes open. We have taken the path of a non-sectarian way of life and stayed away from all kinds of narrow dogmas,' Aruna said confidently.

'That may be true, behan, but why can't the others do the same? Why can't an ordinary person realise this? Surely, what is possible for us is also possible for the man on the street? This is where the crux lies: we need to campaign for a particular kind of education, not the drivel that passes in the name of education. Through textbooks, schools, and colleges, we need to nurture a broader way of thinking among Hindus and Muslims. With the slightest provocation, everything goes up in flames because there is no strong foundation to keep things together. Sensible and rational education can do that. It is so unfortunate that our writers, editors, journalists, teachers—none of them seem to have a greater interest in the health of the nation. If you ask me, we have only regressed in this respect,' Hamid said with frustration.

Vijay interjected, 'Dost, what you say about education and pedagogy is true, but I feel we need to address basic needs first. Our main problem is hunger and sustenance. Nobody wants to hear about education and sermons until their stomachs are full. Try waxing eloquently about the beauties of nature before a starving man. He won't listen to you. To preach to a poor man is mockery if not violence. Hamid, the first need is *jismaani*, the physical, not *ruhaani* or spiritual.'

'So we are circling back to the same thing. We need our own government. When the reins of government are no longer in selfish hands and when people who are committed to employment, education, and justice take the helm, things will improve,' Aruna said.

'But we can be free and autonomous to form our own government only if Hindus and Muslims have *ittehad*—that is, they unite and get along!' Hamid smiled.

'I think inter-religious marriage is the answer. Can you not see? If Hindus and Muslims intermarry, we will be able to remove this poison. A child born of a Hindu father and a Muslim mother, or the other way around, will not become sectarian. How can he reject Hinduism or Islam if both remind him of his parents?' Aruna asked.

'I do agree that matrimonial considerations need to change. The decision to marry should lie with the individuals marrying. They are the ones who have to face unhappiness and go through difficulties. It's all very well for family and relatives to offer suggestions, but they should not control the decision or break ties with a couple should they marry of their own choice.'

'Do you remember how we had to hide and marry because your father was against it? Asha's father was extremely upset with me just because we were born in different communities. It was as if loving and marrying each other was a sin. The entire family turned against us. I find this kind of traditionalism so damaging.' Vijay spoke with agitation.

'Yes, I believe that people should have the freedom to marry. If they make a mistake, they should realise it on their own,' Hamid replied.

'But we need to ensure that there is some fallback system available for women so that they don't miss out on support. It's harder for women. Should the marriage not work out, there should be other alternatives available to them,' Aruna said.

'That's true. I also believe that people should not be expected to change their religion. Neither should a Hindu girl be made to do a *nikaah*, nor should a Muslim man be expected to do a *shuddhi*. Religion is meant to be about spiritual life, not about increasing people's misery. Really, just the thought of hostility and violence in the name of religion makes me feel it's better to have a world without religion!' Hamid added with anger.

'Hamid bhai, if you could put your ideals into action and create a knowledge base, we would be inhabiting a free and secular nation.'

Aruna's words rang in Hamid's ears. He fell silent.

9

Asha was a picture of simplicity, indifferent to the idea of dressing up and looking pretty, no matter how much her mother pleaded with her to wear ornaments. But all of a sudden, she seemed like a different person. She was carefully draping a saree and delicately combing her hair. She seemed interested in life, almost as if she loved herself, as though she considered her life precious. She had awakened to the joys of life, which she now wanted to experience with open arms. Her dormant emotions seemed to have been stirred. Seeing Asha's changed behaviour, Gauri Devi's joy knew no bounds. She eagerly returned to her deities to thank them. She was convinced that a laughing and happy Asha meant that her daughter was ready to marry. But Shankarlal's mind was filled with suspicion, and he had new misgivings. He kept a strict eye on his daughter. He despised the thought of Vijay and Aruna, who, he believed, may have been responsible for something devious. One day, he saw Vijay walking with Hamid. Vijay smiled and greeted him, but Shankarlal frowned with displeasure and turned away to go in the opposite direction.

On witnessing such hatred, Hamid was taken aback. His heartbeat quickened, and a darkness engulfed him. This gentle soul always avoided anger or any kind of misbehaviour. He was willing to make any sacrifice, but he would never compromise his self-respect. He pursed his lips, recalling how rude Asha's father had been. He had also heard a full account from Vijay. Hamid was tempted to turn around and leave Almora forever, but a bird living among the trees of Almora had now captivated his heart. How could he give that up?

The closer Hamid got to his departure, the more restless he became. His heart sank at the thought of not seeing Asha again. It had been many days since he had last met her. He was often tempted to go to the waterfall again to meet her, but the thought of her father restrained him. Day and night he prayed to meet her again, somewhere, somehow. His heart was restive, but his lips were sealed. Finally, the day before his departure arrived. He had only twenty-four hours left. He wondered whether he should confide in Aruna. Meanwhile, Aruna suspected that Hamid was in a state of turmoil. But neither of them had yet become each other's confidants.

As usual, Aruna was preparing to leave to meet Asha.

'Even a devotee would be less committed to his God! How unfailingly you go to have *darshan* of your friend! You have reserved all your days for her. Don't you think poor mortals like us deserve some of your time?'

'Why don't you join me then?'

'And interrupt your friendly natter?'

'I assure you it would be no interruption! I can speak for my friend as well.'

'No, behan, I didn't mean to join you. I just thought if you could join us today instead of going to see your friend.'

'I'd love to, Hamid bhai. But if I don't turn up, Asha will start worrying about me.'

'So much the better then! She will come to check on you.'

'Oh, that didn't occur to me. How clever you are!' Aruna smiled.

Hamid smiled back. His face had turned crimson, but he made no effort to hide it.

10

Hamid felt every moment stretch like a year. The slightest sound of a footstep or a rustle quickened his heartbeat. The gentlest knock on the door sent him into a frenzy. He kept looking out of the window and pacing up and down on the veranda. He could neither bring himself to speak nor to read. Asha was at the centre of his thoughts. Would he meet her at all? He was so lost in his longing that he did not realise when he fell asleep, his book still in his hand. At around 4 pm, he was called for tea. Hamid had barely stepped into the living room when his eyes fell upon Asha. She was filling the teacups. When did she arrive and through which door? He couldn't believe his eyes. Was she really there or was she just a figment of his imagination? It was only when Asha looked up and smiled at him that he believed it to be true. His face lit up with joy. He found his voice and asked, 'When did you come?'

'At least an hour ago. You were so lost in reading your book that you didn't notice me.'

'I was definitely lost but not in the book,' Hamid said wistfully.

'Oh! You must be missing Sindh then,' Asha responded.

'Not at all. There is only one thing I miss: a ray of hope, an asha. Will this hope be fulfilled, I wonder.' Hamid's voice was filled with sadness.

'You missed this hope so much that you forgot to say goodbye to Asha.' Asha feigned anger.

'But I have not been apart from Asha, so how could I...?' Hamid smiled.

Asha was about to say something, but Aruna and Vijay appeared, so she stopped herself. Hamid also changed his facial expression and asked Vijay, 'Who were you talking to?'

'Brij Kishore, the secretary of Harijan *basti*, the colony of untouchables. He is a hardworking man of impeccable integrity. He is like a god to the Harijans. He has created such awareness that no one dares to oppress the Harijans any more. If I were to show you the homes in the *basti*, you would see how neat and clean they are. A week ago, Asha's father hit a sanitation worker over some trivial issue. All the sanitation workers united and decided to boycott his home. Finally, he had to admit his mistake and convey his apology through Brij Kishore.

Only then did the sanitation workers agree to clean his home.'

'Really, the most marginalised will be valued when they make others realise the power of their labour and mind,' Hamid said.

'Hamid bhai, ever since the Harijans and other oppressed groups have made their collectives, Shankarlal and his cronies have been very upset with us,' Aruna said.

'When people are about to lose dominance, they will react,' Hamid said.

Suddenly Aruna's eyes fell upon Asha's saree. She squealed, '*Arre* Asha! You are wearing a khadi saree today!'

'It doesn't look like khadi. It looks like silk,' Asha said mischievously.

'Are you not allowed to even wear a khadi saree?' Hamid asked incredulously.

'My father thinks khadi reeks of rebellion.' Asha laughed.

'Parents always want children to flourish and grow but often expect them to do so in their own image,' Hamid teased.

'But nature produces its fruits for everyone. It doesn't impose the same conditions that parents do,' Asha said, looking into Hamid's eyes.

'If human beings were to be students of nature, God knows how far we would go,' Hamid remarked.

'If humans don't learn from nature's laws, they'll surely learn the hard way. Nature is merciless and will exact its price,' Aruna added.

'Nature is certainly just, but it is not devoid of mercy. Otherwise, we would not be forgiven time and again, and all our endeavours would come to naught,' Asha said.

'Bhai, can we stop with the heavy philosophising so we can have our tea peacefully?' Vijay said with exasperation.

'Alright, are we allowed to talk about Harijans and Gandhi then?' Hamid laughed.

'No, no, we need to finish our tea quickly and drop Asha safely home,' Aruna said.

Hamid and Asha exchanged a glance. There was fear and pain in their eyes.

Part II

11

Gulu took the telegram from the postman and rushed to his mother. Excited at the thought of news from his elder brother, Hamid, Gulu was almost out of breath. Panting, he asked his mother, 'Amma, just check if the telegram is from bhai. Tell me, when is he coming?' Even Zarina came running. Their mother read the telegram and said, 'This evening. He arrives by Punjab Express.' Gulu put his arms around his mother and said, 'Amma I will definitely go to the station to receive him.' Zarina chimed in, 'Me too, Amma!' Their mother told Gulu, 'Go and show this telegram to your father, and tell him to take both of you along to the station.' Umed Ali read the telegram and entered Roshan Ara's room. Looking sheepish, he said, 'I don't think I'll be able to go to pick up Hamid.'

'Why? What are you busy with?' Roshan Ara asked politely.

'I have to visit Pir Sain in the evening. Why don't you take the kids and go to the station? The car is available. I'll walk to the Pir's place.'

Roshan Ara was irritated by her husband's response, but she knew there was no point in saying anything. No good would come out of it. Umed Ali heeded his wife's advice when it came to worldly matters, but when it came to spiritual matters, he was adamant. He considered her inexperienced in this regard. Ever since his retirement, he spent all his time among Sufi pirs and fakirs. His entire focus was on the worship of God, and he kept away from all social relations and responsibilities. His wife did not like this otherworldly life her husband had adopted. Though she was a person of faith herself, she was convinced that God was best served through His people. She believed that our first duty was to serve the *mulk*, the nation we lived in. To her, his behaviour seemed like indifference, almost treacherous to the nation. Umed Ali felt that rationality was a hindrance to spiritual accomplishment, whereas Roshan Ara thought the opposite. She felt that if God had bestowed the mind, it was to assist in the accomplishment of both worldly and otherworldly goals. The mind was not inimical to the soul; rather, it was its companion. To sideline rationality or turn away from social responsibilities was cowardice, as far as Roshan Ara was concerned. Despite such differences between husband and wife, there was harmony in their conjugal life. They did not distrust each other, rather they respected each other's views, and that's why theirs was a happy home, filled with joy and merriment.

12

Roshan Ara, Gulu, and Zarina got ready in the evening and rushed to the car to head to the station. The children were so eager to see their brother that every moment felt unbearably long. Upon reaching the station, they went to the train and searched every second-class compartment, but they could not find Hamid. They looked at each other with disappointment. Just then, they heard Hamid's voice. They saw him getting down from a third-class compartment. Gulu squealed with delight. Hamid touched his mother's feet and hugged his siblings. Roshan Ara embraced her son, saying, 'It was foolish of you to travel by third class in this heat. All the rest and rejuvenation you received in the hills must have vanished now!'

Hamid smiled and said, 'The third class provided more entertaining company than the second class.' Not seeing his father at the station, Hamid asked his mother. She replied with some resentment, 'When will he think of his children if his life continues to be occupied by murshids?'

'Amma, how does Baba spend his time now that he has retired?' Hamid asked.

'The murshid conveyed the famous words of Shah Abdul Latif: "Learn the letter of the soul, forget all other books." So, he is in a state of forgetting. If he can't remember the world in the present, he is hardly going to remember the past.' Roshan Ara chuckled. She had her son's luggage picked up, and they all headed towards the car.

'That's fine, too, as long as he writes about this Sufi philosophy. Never mind remembering the rest. He can share this wisdom with the world.'

'He thinks the mind must be forgotten to connect with spirituality. But if the mind is used, where would all the pirs and murshids go? How would they survive?'

Roshan Ara had barely finished when Gulu announced, 'We are home! We are home!'

Hamid alighted from the car. Zarina held his hand and asked, 'Bhai, which of the two is better: Karachi or Lucknow?'

Hamid hugged her and said, 'Zarina is better than both.'

Gulu got out of the car and went to bring his friend, Ranjit, to meet Hamid. He proudly held Ranjit's hand and said, 'This is my elder brother. He's a professor at a college in Lucknow. He's very intelligent and always stood first in his class.'

Hamid laughed uproariously on seeing his brother brag like this and said, 'When will you stand first, you braggart?' Then Hamid turned to Ranjit and asked, 'Putta, which one of you is more intelligent: you or Gulu?'

Shyly, Ranjit lowered his eyes and replied, 'Zarina is more intelligent than either of us. She always stands first. She even received an award this year. I stood third, and Gulu came tenth.'

'*Wah re bhai, wah!*' Hamid poked Gulu. 'You are a star!'

A sheepish Gulu hid his face in his mother's lap, 'I was unwell this year. Ask Amma.'

'Child, are you older or Gulu?' Hamid asked Ranjit. Even Ranjit was keen to be asked this, and he replied with alacrity, 'I am older, of course. I was born in 1932. I am in Zarina's class. I will be taking the Senior Cambridge exam next year.'

'Oh, really? Whose son are you? What does your father do?' Hamid asked.

'My father is Uttamchand Advani,' Ranjit replied proudly. 'He is a doctor.'

While Hamid was still chatting with the kids, Umed Ali entered the room. He embraced his son. He was proud of him and was convinced that Hamid was no ordinary person.

13

After his retirement, Umed Ali had purchased a new house at Kemps Road in Karachi. Dr Uttamchand Advani was his neighbour. The two of them had become good friends, almost like brothers. Uttamchand had also become a follower of Umed Ali's Sufi mentor. He, too, believed in the community of Sufi followers, the *sangat* of spirituality. After his wife's death, he lost interest in social affairs. Had it not been for the two children his wife had left behind, he would have happily gone to the banks of the Ganga and spent his life in *bhakti*. His daughter, Mohini, had completed her Bachelor's degree and was now a married woman. She used to take care of Ranjit, and Uttamchand hoped that she would continue to do so even after marriage. But such was his misfortune that his daughter's marriage only increased his problems, instead of setting him free.

A young man named Mohan Shivdasani worked as Uttamchand's assistant. Mohan was a modest and ethical person and had made a deep impression on him. As a result, Uttamchand entrusted many responsibilities to Mohan, who had managed to earn the trust of all the patients. Such was Uttamchand's faith in this young man that he wanted Mohan to become his son-in-law. When Mohini learnt of her father's intentions, she rebelled, saying, 'Mohan is dark and wears khadi. I don't want this kind of a man. I would like a good-looking man with a foreign degree.' Dr Uttamchand was a strong opponent of the dowry system, the *deti-leti*, but made helpless by his daughter's desire, he compromised on his principles and gave a dowry of □15,000 to the man Mohini wanted to marry. Mohini's husband, Arjun Sitlani, was a suave and good-looking man, always dressed in a suit and boots. He worked with the Tata company in Bombay. Mohini was overjoyed by his looks and success and felt there was no one more fortunate than herself. She moved to Bombay soon after marriage, but her happiness did not last long. Arjun was addicted to alcohol and was in a relationship with a Christian woman. Mohini tried her best to pull him away from his addiction. She made efforts to lure him towards her with entreaties and threats—anything to bring him around. However, things only worsened. He told her that wives had no business keeping an eye on their husbands. But Mohini was not a timid woman. She waited for a year somehow. But once she bore a child, she had had enough. Her little daughter was born with poor vision, so Mohini brought her to her father's home. Uttamchand informed her that the child was congenitally blind. Mohini felt that the child was paying the price for her father's debauched life and was filled with loathing towards her husband. She wanted nothing more to do with him. Meanwhile, the little girl passed away within a month. Mohini severed her relationship with her husband and returned to her father's home forever. An agonised Uttamchand watched his daughter's world collapse. He was far too dignified to remind her of the mistakes she had made, so he now strove to assuage her misery and support her.

Initially, Mohini refused to come out of her room. She did not talk to her friends or mingle with anybody, but gradually, thanks to her father's efforts and Mohan's kindness, things somewhat changed. She shed her preoccupation with looks and wealth and began to value Mohan's authenticity. She began to think of him with affection and respect. But how was the chasm between them going to disappear? It was perhaps too late.

14

'Hamid, Inayat Ali's letter arrived just yesterday. I don't understand what I should say to him. Your mother explained the entire matter to you, and you mentioned in your letter that we would discuss this in person. Now, what is your view on this?' Umed Ali asked.

This sudden question from his father was a jolt to Hamid. He didn't know where to start. The answer was clear in his mind, but his father was not going to like it. Hamid could not think of a ruse that would help avoid the matter once again, but the thought of the impact his reply would have made him nervous. Hamid waited a couple of minutes, then finally looked respectfully into his father's eyes and said, 'I have not yet made plans to marry.'

Roshan Ara responded to her son with patience, 'If you do intend to marry eventually, why waste away your best years? What is the point?'

'And what would be the point of marrying if I don't feel the need to?' Hamid replied, amused. 'Even books provide me with companionship!'

'This means that Shireen is not acceptable to you,' Roshan Ara declared.

'I have nothing against her. In fact, I would go to the extent of saying that the man who marries someone as good as her would be lucky. But I apologise, I am not that person. She deserves someone better,' Hamid said politely.

'What rubbish! The girl is pining for you, dreaming about you, and you are saying you don't deserve her?' Roshan Ara objected.

'That's what I am saying, *na*. If I don't value a girl like her, that means I don't deserve her!' Hamid smiled.

'Enough with these excuses. They are unnecessary and a rather sly way of avoiding the matter. So just tell us the truth,' Roshan Ara spoke in a measured tone.

'What if you don't like my truth...?' Hamid teased her.

'Well, what can I possibly do if I don't like your truth? You can choose to please me, or please yourself. I can hardly rule your life.' Roshan Ara's voice betrayed resentment.

'So you are allowing me the freedom to please myself, right?'

'Whether or not I allow it, what difference does that make? These days, only parents bear the onus of fulfilling their duties,' his mother said wistfully.

Hamid laughed. 'That's it, Amma? You have already given up on me?'

'If children don't understand their duties, what can parents do?' she replied.

Hamid dropped the flippant tone. 'I am sorry, but allow me to express my opinion honestly. I don't think marriages are duties that parents need to worry about. There are duties and responsibilities we owe to ourselves.'

On hearing her son's pointed answer, Roshan Ara lacked the courage to press the matter further. She fell silent. Hamid noticed his mother's withdrawal. Softening his tone, he said to her, 'Amma, why are you quiet? Tell me, if a decision makes you happy but makes me unhappy, would that be acceptable to you?'

'No, my child. My days are limited. It's your life and your turn to blossom. If you are happy, I am happy,' Roshan Ara said.

'So are you giving me the freedom to be happy?' Hamid asked.

Roshan Ara looked into Hamid's eyes. 'Now share with us, what is going on? What is your desire? Stop beating around the bush. Open your heart to us.'

Hamid blushed. Should he tell them? Finally, he mustered up the courage and said, 'Amma, I have lost my heart to someone.'

'To whom? When? Is there someone waiting for you in the mountains of Almora?' Roshan Ara asked in disbelief.

Hamid smiled and answered in the affirmative.

'But who is she? Tell us.' His mother became impatient.

'Khuda's creation!' Hamid smiled, but his face was serious.

'We are all Khuda's creations. But what's her name? Her family? *Jaat-paat*?'

'*Jaat-paat?* Do you believe in the dogmas of caste and community?'

Roshan Ara took a deep breath and paused. If she showed any disapproval at this stage, she may lose her son's confidence. She had always said that it was more important for hearts to meet rather than castes. Little did she realise that it's easy to offer such platitudes but so difficult to put them into practice. Torn between her ideals and the practical imperatives of real life, Roshan Ara did not know what to say. She mustered her courage, almost bit her lower lip, and said, 'Regardless of my belief in caste and creed, few would dispute the fact that relations forged within one's own community bring greater joy than those with another community.'

'Granted, in this atmosphere of intolerance, it is difficult for parents to accept unions that transcend caste differences,' Hamid said.

'So, which relationship can exist without involving parents? And especially one that displeases them? In which heaven or earth are such relationships to take place?' Umed Ali asked with irritation.

'Well, as I've mentioned before, I believe that marriage is more a matter for the individual than a duty to the parents,' Hamid replied firmly.

Roshan Ara realised that this was not the right moment to express her consternation. That would prevent her from knowing what was going on in Hamid's mind. So, she changed tack. 'Alright, putta. Never mind the different ways of seeing this issue or the fact that you have already selected the girl. At least tell us which community she is from, Hindu, Parsi, or European?'

'Hindu,' Hamid replied.

Upon hearing his son's reply, Umed Ali was immediately agitated. 'A Hindu girl? Absolutely not! You are foolish if you think a Hindu parent will want an alliance with a Muslim family. This kind of match is doomed to fail.'

'Perhaps it may. But these are conflicts between the old times and the new. I don't see anything unusual in this matter.'

'As long as Hindus continue to be arrogant about their Hinduness, do you think they would be ready to accept Islam?'

'But I don't understand why anyone should be coerced into changing their religion? Everyone's personhood is a product of the many contexts from which they come. Religion is an individual's personal matter and faith. Problems arise when people are forced to convert.'

'But how will a Hindu girl remain Hindu after marrying a Muslim? She is, after all, the wife of a Muslim man, right? That's her identity.' Umed Ali's eyes glinted with rage.

'What is Hindu? What is Muslim? Frankly, I am not able to see any fundamental difference between the two. I don't understand why Hindus and Muslims react this way when they hear about each other. Hindus and Muslims could potentially share so much more with each other than they might find difficult to share with their own co-religionists. If spiritual and intellectual companionship were encouraged in religious matters, such unions could be possible.'

'Never mind how much intimacy exists between two people—whether of an intellectual or spiritual kind—unless they share the same religion, there cannot be a real union between them,' Umed Ali declared emphatically.

'I don't understand. What do you consider "religion"? If religion means spiritual evolution, I don't see why a Hindu or Muslim cannot achieve compatibility. However, if the meaning of religion is bloodshed and skirmishes, I believe that such a dangerous phenomenon as religion must be annihilated once and for all. Honestly, this sectarianism has rendered us so blind that we are unable to distinguish an inferior person from a superior one without thinking of religion first. In my view, India will prosper and survive only once religious fervour has been made a crime.'

Roshan Ara noticed how agitated her son had become. She put her own reservations aside and said, 'You are right, putta. What you say is true. However, we also live in a society and have a duty to live by its norms, don't you think? It is also expected of us to maintain the dignity of our religion.'

'Certainly, if it is beneficial and serves the greater good. However, if the dignity of religion causes harm to the individual or the nation, I don't see why it should exist. I also believe that individuals can and should sacrifice their comforts and luxuries for the greater good of humanity, but if religion goes against humanity, why should it exist in the first place? Why cling to illiterate dogmas?'

'You are the only Muslim who would give his wife the freedom to pursue her religion,' Umed Ali said with resentment.

'Those who are not able to respect another person's religion have no right to marry outside their religion. Sufism also does not teach us such discrimination. The dharma of Sufism is to embrace all religions. If a Hindu can become a disciple of a Muslim pir and does not feel the need to change his religion, why are these conversions necessary for marriage? I firmly believe that all religions have more in common with each other than we acknowledge. They are all fundamentally committed to the same credo. Both Islam and Hinduism emphasise annihilating the self to become an image of divinity.'

'Putta, what you say is absolutely right. But the point is, it's very difficult to turn away from existing practices, from *maryada*.' Roshan Ara looked at her son ruefully.

'But Amma, *maryada* or customary honour also changes with time—and it must. Rivers remain sacred as long as they keep flowing. If they are not allowed to flow, the water will rise like an angry tide or create filth and odour. Our country's highest priority right now is to stop making distinctions of caste and creed so that others cannot take advantage of this. Otherwise, these domestic fights will assume such demonic forms that it's terrifying to think about how much we would regret them later.'

'But how can a union between Hindus and Muslims take place if a Hindu considers himself purer than a Muslim and finds the idea of even dining with a Muslim loathsome? If Hindus continue to practice untouchability and despise Muslims, why would Muslims not harbour contempt and seek opportunities to avenge the insults?' Roshan Ara said with agitation.

Hamid listened to his mother carefully and responded, 'You are right, Amma. Hindus definitely suffer from this terrible malady of untouchability. But they don't do this only to Muslims; they also do this to their own brethren. I think this pernicious habit stems from their misplaced sense of hygiene. Hinduism has placed a lot of emphasis on hygiene and sanitation, which is why you will notice that even the poorest Hindu will bathe every day and cook and clean.'

'But that does not mean that they should despise others and give a religious tinge to ordinary things like cleanliness. Europeans are cleaner than Hindus, but the latter look down upon them as well,' Roshan Ara said.

'No doubt, Hindus, in particular, suffer from the malaise of untouchability. By doing this, they think they are being faithful to their religion. I believe that Hindus are bringing a bad name to their religion by doing so. Like our Muslims bring a bad name to Islam with their dogmas. But I don't blame either Hinduism or Islam for it. This has to do with illiteracy, which is inevitable in such a large country. Once people are awakened to a new way of thinking, these things will go away. This will happen only when we cease to live under a foreign government. Only complaints and arguments will not help us abolish such backward thinking. The ones who consider themselves educated and broadminded need to show more understanding, generosity, and wisdom.'

While mother and son were still arguing, Gulu came running inside. 'Amma, read this news! Such a terrifying incident took place in Dadu! Eight Muslim men went around with swords, slaughtered a Hindu landowner, confiscated his wealth, and took away his young wife.' Turning to his brother, Gulu asked, 'Bhai, why do Muslims cause this bloodshed? Are they so merciless?'

'Uncivilised people like these have no scruples. People become beasts when they are hungry and deprived. Whenever they see wealth, they think they have a right to lay their hands on it.'

'So why does the government keep its subjects hungry and unemployed? The king has a duty to keep his subjects happy. Our teacher told us that the king is benevolent and just,' Gulu said.

'Your teacher's king may be benevolent in England but not in India. Most Indians are uneducated, and many of them don't have food to eat.'

'Is that why the king of England rules over us? Why do we live under foreign rule?'

'Because we lack strength and unity. Because Hindus and Muslims keep fighting with each other. Haven't you heard the story about two cats fighting over a piece of sweet? They go to a monkey, who ends up eating the sweet, and the cats are left with nothing.'

'How foolish of the cats!'

'The British are also sly, like the monkey. Hindus and Muslims go to them for arbitration over every small thing.'

'Does the Englishman make them reconcile with each other?'

'Reconcile? Far from it. The Englishman makes it worse by driving a wedge between them so that he can claim neither of them is ready for self-rule.'

'Is that why Gandhiji says that when Hindus and Muslims unite, *swaraj* will be achieved? But our Christian teacher says that Gandhiji is very ungrateful. The English have brought such good things to India, yet he keeps fighting with them.'

'What does your teacher say? Which good things?' Hamid probed.

'He says that the English brought machinery to India, which led to the establishment of mills and factories. And that they also built trains. Before that, people used to travel on camels and donkeys. They introduced electricity, whereas earlier, Indians used to light lamps. Electricity has made cooking gas possible, and there are fans to get rid of the heat. Look at how much entertainment is available because of the radio, with news from anywhere in the world. And the cinema halls—just think of all the fun they provide! All these comforts were not possible before the British, right?'

'But you know, India was prosperous and happy even without all these technologies and comforts, and now, even with all this machinery, India is hungry and deprived,' Hamid explained.

'Then why are we not getting rid of the British? We study in geography that India has a population of 35 crores. Can so many people not manage to handle a few Britishers?' Gulu asked incredulously.

'Yes, of course, we are a large population, but people don't get along with each other.'

'Right. We also study that there is strength in unity. When I grow up, bhai, I will teach Hindus and Muslims to unite, to do *ittehad*.' Gulu's chest swelled with pride.

15

Hamid read Vijay's letter and fell into deep thought. He was saddened to learn about the sudden death of Shankarlal, but he also saw a ray of hope in this development. Asha's father had unleashed his wrath upon a servant over a trivial issue. He had a weak heart, and the agitation led to heart failure. After his death, Vijay and Aruna spent a few days at Gauri Devi's house. They organised all the matters related to money and inheritance and then brought Asha and Gauri Devi to Allahabad.

The sudden loss of her father left a void in Asha's heart, but it also freed her from many anxieties. There were no more shackles around her. She no longer had to fear anyone. She felt as if she had been reborn. She joined Aruna in social upliftment activities. Vijay hired a tutor to teach her English at home. Asha felt that given the current climate in India, it was important to learn the language. As such, English was not entirely new to her. Whenever

Aruna got an opportunity, she would tutor Asha in the language while sitting by the waterfall in Almora. It was all done in secret, but the two friends managed to both teach and learn. This was also why Aruna made sure they met almost every day.

Meanwhile, Asha worked on social upliftment for about a month, but the work failed to absorb her. The peace and fulfilment she craved was not to be found in this work. Moreover, city life did not attract her. Her heart pined for a quieter environment. Having grown up amidst nature's beauty, how could the hustle and bustle of a city provide her peace? Her despondency disturbed Vijay. He had taken it upon himself to ensure she was safe and happy.

During those days, some of Aruna's friends had gone to Rabindranath Tagore's ashram, Shantiniketan, to learn art and music. Seeing Asha's inclination towards the arts, Aruna wished to send her to Shantiniketan. However, she wondered if Gauri Devi would permit it and reined in her enthusiasm. The question was how to even bring this up with Gauri Devi.

Hamid had visited Shantiniketan several times, so Aruna and Vijay found it useful to seek his advice on the matter before broaching the subject with Asha's mother. Hamid was overjoyed at the thought of Asha in Shantiniketan, which had a special place in his heart. Whenever Vijay met him, Hamid would make sure to bring up Shantiniketan in the conversation.

He considered it an ideal expression of education and refinement in India. It was where the soul of India lived, he believed, and it showed the way to a new India. It had the promise of becoming a pilgrimage for all religions and communities—such was its modernity. He marvelled at how people from all walks of life came to this ashram and learnt from each other without giving up their distinct identities.

Hamid felt that Asha's unexpressed longing for nature and poetry would find an outlet in Shantiniketan. The place would also provide her solace and the freedom to shed her inhibitions, both personally and intellectually. She would find the courage to express her views and gain confidence. Vijay was extremely comforted and thrilled to receive Hamid's encouraging letter. He immediately established contact with Shantiniketan and got Asha enrolled in a programme of art and music. Now the question was how to make Gauri Devi agree to the plan. Aruna broached the subject with her, and although Gauri Devi did not like the idea of sending a young daughter away, she relented after much persuasion from Asha. She loved her daughter too much to see her unhappy. Vijay and Aruna praised the ashram highly and assured her of Asha's safety and happiness. Once the vacation was over, Vijay himself took Asha to the ashram, handed her over to Aruna's friends and returned home.

Asha's joy knew no bounds in Shantiniketan. She felt as if she was returning to her roots, to her home.

This was exactly the kind of life she had dreamt of ever since she was a child. Her dream was finally coming true, and she blossomed like a flower. When she strolled through the grounds of Shantiniketan, singing to herself or frolicking with her friends, she felt her life was blissful. Only caged birds, once free, know how it feels to spread their wings in the sky and fly across the firmament with joy and fearlessness.

Asha's sweet demeanour won many a heart at Shantiniketan. Her heartrending voice had made her the favourite of every ashramite. She was both liked and respected by the old and the young. Yet, the attention had not made her smug; rather, she went through life with humility. Her smile wiped away people's anger and worries, and before long, Asha had made a profound impact on the people of Shantiniketan.

16

This time, Hamid did not feel exasperated in Sindh. He spent time with the kind of company he liked and began to form ties with the doctor's family. He particularly liked Dr Mohan and found their friendship enriching—both intellectually and emotionally. The two of them chatted for hours. Where hearts and minds meet, can caste and communal differences matter? Honestly, *ruhaani* or spiritual companionship can help transcend all differences, and there were many examples of this kind of togetherness in Sindh. Hamid's strong reservations about the Sindhi community began to fade. To him, Mohan seemed like a ray of hope—a picture of ideals and principles in a newly emerging India. His compassion and intelligence were remarkable. Hamid was also astonished to see the radical change in Mohini's life. The once-spoilt rich girl had transformed into a revolutionary. The society that had misled Mohini into thinking of women's roles in narrow ways and created the Mohini of the past was now under her critique. Mohini had started speaking out to address women, so that they would not be misled as she once had been. She spearheaded a campaign to abolish the practice of *deti-leti* or dowry. Her pamphlets and lectures were fiery, and she threatened to report people demanding dowry to the police. To uproot this evil practice, everything had to be done. She had gathered a small army of young men and women who were against the dowry system. People asking or giving dowries were exposed and feared arrest and public shaming.

In matters of *deti-leti,* Mohan was Mohini's companion and collaborator. With his help, she had become a campaigner. Mohan was a firm believer in women's rights. He believed that unless women claimed their strength and confidence, India's progress would only be a mirage. The most profound influence on a child, in his view, was that of the mother. Therefore, the atmosphere at home, or even the behaviour of teachers at school, had to change first to create self-aware citizens. In Mohan's just mind, women had been rendered helpless as part of a larger structural economy and patriarchy. Religion also played a role in this. Women were made to feel scared of fathers, husbands, and even sons in their old age. This conviction led Mohan to take careful steps. He egged Mohini on and reminded her that men had to learn to give up their power, or at the very least, share it. Men had to stop thinking that only they could earn. Under the guise of distributing free medicines, he would visit the *bastis* of Harijans and workers to spread the message of equality. What he earned from the rich, he spent on the poor. It was his dream that not a single person should remain dependent on the rich or the upper castes. He condemned inequality and domination and had managed to find a place in the hearts of his poor patients.

Mohini's visibility and success, and her companionship with Mohan, set many tongues wagging. The matter was brought to the attention of her husband, Arjun. In his arrogance, Arjun came to Sindh to teach Mohini a lesson. He offered to mentor her. Mohini's response was blunt: 'A husband who could not perform his duty as my protector cannot now claim to be interested in my welfare. I can do well without him.' Arjun was enraged, and it didn't help matters that he 'saw' Mohini with another man. But Mohini had begun to spread her wings, so even though Arjun was being instigated by his friends to take her to court, he knew little good would come of it. Helpless and angry, he returned to Bombay and began living with someone else. It mattered little to Mohini.

Suddenly, one day, Ranjit brought the newspaper to Mohini. It stated that Arjun had met with a fatal accident and had died. Mohini was shocked. Although she had no love or affection for him, her tender heart still ached. She prayed for his soul to find peace.

17

'You look quite downcast these days. Why is that?' Umed Ali asked his wife.

Roshan Ara sighed, 'Well, if you had to endure all these problems alone, what else could be expected? I ...'

'Alone, did you say? I am here, well and alive. Why would you have to face anything alone? Share it with me.'

'What's the point of confiding in you? You'll just tell me to leave it to fate and the Almighty.'

Umed Ali laughed. 'Tell me, isn't that true? Doesn't divine will govern us all? It is Allah's wish.'

Roshan Ara spoke with irritation, 'Of course, there's no point in using one's brain. No effort needs to be made. Just abdicate all responsibility, and blame it on fate. What is the difference between humans and non-humans if no effort is to be made? I understand that success is not entirely in our hands, but *himmat-e-mardaan, madad-e-Khuda*. If no effort is made, even God cannot help.'

'Let's not argue over this. Tell me, what is bothering you?'

'I am really worried about Zarina. Honestly, it was better to have child marriages.'

'But what is the matter? You were the one against child marriages. You advocated education and degrees. Why are you talking like this today?'

'I was hopeful that I would be free of her responsibility once Hamid got married. Zarina would no longer be my headache. But man proposes, and God disposes.' Roshan Ara spoke with sadness.

'That's exactly what I am saying. Humans are helpless.'

'Why helpless? If one door closes, another opens.'

'Alright, look for another door. We know that Hamid's door is closed,' Umed Ali said with sarcasm.

'Of course, I will. I want to send Zarina to my brothers in Aligarh. I don't think it's safe to keep her here.'

'But why send the child away from under your own supervision? It's best to keep an eye on children. We can influence them then. Look at what an unfaithful man Hamid has turned out to be. It's all the result of us sending him away. You know what he told me today? I asked him to join me in paying respects to Pir saheb. He said, "My God does not live amongst the pirs; he lives in the hearts of the poor. I don't need this grace." I am quite clear that I will not send Gulu away from me, lest he also becomes a rebel.'

Roshan Ara could not bear Hamid being criticised. 'You will value Hamid when the world considers him a hero. Hamid is the closest to Allah. But never mind, I was talking about Zarina. Why bring Hamid into the picture?'

'I don't see any merit in sending Zarina anywhere. I don't know why you want to do this,' Umed Ali said.

'If you were paying attention to matters at home, you would not be asking this. You are absorbed in your own world.'

'But what are you trying to say?'

'I do not like the closeness between Ranjit and Zarina. They can't seem to live without each other.'

'Have you gone mad? They are just kids busy with school matters. You are speculating unnecessarily.' Umed Ali was shocked.

'Yes, they are busy with school matters. They are innocent now. But who is to tell what will happen once they become adults? Hamid's decision will influence Zarina, but I will not tolerate my girl marrying outside Islam. If Zarina marries a Hindu, it's just unthinkable! I have to keep her away from Ranjit. It's sinful.'

'If you find this sinful, why would you not consider Hamid marrying a Hindu girl sinful or the fact that she may have to embrace Islam? Anyway, Allah's wishes must be respected. But I still insist that you do not let Zarina be far from you. Use love and kindness to keep her under your control. A mother's influence can work on her.'

'I will try my best, but it may come to nothing. Unless she is separated from Ranjit, little good will come of anything. You should have seen her yesterday. Ranjit was unwell, so Zarina didn't eat all day. She wandered around looking sick and worried. It's best to nip this in the bud.'

'Well, it's up to you then. Do what your mind and spirit tell you to do. I just want to remind you that a mother has a bigger claim on her children compared to the father.'

'I could have sent her to Lucknow to stay with Amma, but I fear that Hamid's influence may not be good for her. And my brother is such a strict disciplinarian, so Aligarh seems like the best choice. Even Khurshid's company will be good for her.'

'But Hamid is not going to be in Lucknow.'

'Now where is he going?'

'Towards Russia—Samarkand and Bukhara. He wants to travel through the countries of the Soviet Union. He's only dreaming of that communist world now. Anyway, let's see what Allah wishes. The world is facing another war, and times are going to be hard. Our pirs and fakirs have already predicted this.'

'Pirs and fakirs or our own common sense? People acquainted with historical developments can also predict that the world is going to witness bloodshed and destruction.'

18

It broke Ranjit's heart to see Zarina in tears. He asked her, 'Why are you crying?' His eyes were moist. 'Did the teacher say anything? Have you not done your homework?'

Zarina wiped her eyes. 'My mother is sending me to Aligarh to my uncle's place.'

Ranjit responded sweetly, 'So what is the problem, Zarina? It's always good to get away from home. I'd love to go away. You know, when children living far away return to their homes, they receive so much love and attention. I will also come with you. I can't survive here without you.'

'But I don't like my Amma's brother. In fact, he does not like Hindus. He is very dogmatic. He says Hindus are infidels, *kaafirs*. He doesn't even allow me to read English books. He says only to read the Quran. He makes his wife wear the burqa. He will not even let me talk to you.'

Ranjit's eyes widened with fear. 'So aren't you going to Lucknow then?'

'I would have loved to go to Hamid bhai, but Amma is not letting me visit him. Bhai is so sweet. He lets us play anything, and he tells us about new and interesting things. He never gets angry. But Amma and Abba don't like his ways. You know, he's probably marrying a Hindu girl. Amma and Abba are very upset, so Amma is not sending me to him.'

'Hindus and Muslims can't marry each other or what?' Ranjit asked, surprised.

'Allah knows. Abba says marrying into another caste is a sin. It makes God angry.'

'Angry? When did he see God? I have not seen Him.'

'Not everyone can see God. Only those who do *Khuda's* prayer, the *bandagi*, and live in His fear, can manage to see God.'

'My father says the same thing. But I have no desire to see God, nor do I know how to pray. One time, my father made a deal with me. He said that if I prayed all night, he would buy me a watch. I prayed all night, and when I saw Baba waking up in the morning, I pretended I was still praying. But you know, while I was praying, I had a dream. It was quite beautiful, though there was no God in it.'

'Won't you tell me your dream? I tell you everything.' Zarina persuaded Ranjit.

'But do you promise not to laugh at me?'

'I promise, I won't.'

'Alright. In my dream, you and I were up in the sky, sitting in an airplane.'

'*Arre wah*! How wonderful! Just imagine if this dream comes true, Ranjit! We could go to Europe then. I've always wanted to visit Europe. You'll come with me, won't you?'

'How can I come with you? You're already leaving me. You won't remember me in Aligarh.' Ranjit dissolved into tears.

'Why would I not remember you? Absence will make the heart grow fonder. Don't I miss bhai when he's away?'

'You'll find girls to be with, no matter how much I miss you. We'll see who forgets the other first—me or you.'

'Oh, here comes bhai.'

They saw Hamid approaching them. He looked happy to see the children.

'What are you two up to, naughty children?' Hamid asked lovingly.

'Bhai,' Zarina said, holding his arm tightly, 'Amma is sending me to Mama's place in Aligarh. Bhai, take me with you, please. I want to go with you.' Zarina's face was pitiable.

Hamid was very attached to his sister, and he knew why Zarina was being sent away. However, he had already hurt his mother and did not feel that he could intervene in this matter. He could not say anything to his mother—at least, not for a while.

19

Hamid's vacation was coming to an end. As the day of his departure drew near, Roshan Ara began to feel a sense of despair. She was extremely attached to her son. While she did not find his rebellion and callousness acceptable, she respected his honesty, courage, and integrity. Beyond a point, she did not push him. Hamid knew that, and therefore, he tried his best not to offend her. He also knew that his mother was a wise and gracious woman who would not let their differences come in the way of his happiness. This time, however, a chasm had developed between mother and son. Hamid had let his mother down, but what could he possibly do? He could not be blamed, but neither could she. As for his father, Hamid knew that despite his protests, he would not leave Hamid's side. He would consider everything *Rab ki raza* and accept the divine will behind all occurrences. So Hamid was not unduly worried about his marriage or the role his parents would play. What bothered him was Asha's mother, Gauri Devi. She came from a different world, which was much more conservative. She would be devasted to learn that her daughter was to marry a Muslim. But she could not be blamed either. She had spent her life in such a small and sheltered world that any change sent her into a state of despair. Hamid was reluctant to be the reason for her heartbreak. He was much too tender and sensitive to build his happiness upon someone else's unhappiness. These thoughts ailed him, and that's why he was glad that Asha was away at Shantiniketan.

That being said, Hamid was deeply affected by his separation from Asha. After returning from Almora, he felt like an outsider everywhere. Even his own home seemed transitory. He couldn't wait to start his own life. But the prospect of going to Russia lifted his spirits. He had been nursing this desire for years, and the present moment seemed better than any other. His father did not approve of the idea, but he did not stop him. His mother was terrified at the thought of her son going so far away. Tears streamed down her face as she imagined the vast distance between them. Even Lucknow had once seemed far. But she knew that her son had a resolute will, and once he made up his mind, there was little that could make him stay behind, so she did not stop him.

She simply asked, 'Will you go alone or with someone?' He replied, 'Alone.' She had assumed that Hamid was planning to go on a honeymoon to Russia.

20

It was Hamid's last day in Sindh, and he felt like buying some special gifts for Asha. He knew she loved all kinds of aesthetic knick-knacks, and Sindh's rural crafts were renowned worldwide. It was amazing that the rural people of Sindh, who lived in arid lands, created such colourful crafts. The handcrafted toys, intricate embroidery, and sculptures were remarkable. Hamid sat on the *pingo*, the swing, and marvelled at the woodwork. Inspired, he decided to go out and do some shopping. He waited at the bus stop for what seemed like an eternity, but there was no sign of a bus. Sweating in the heat, he finally learnt from a passerby that the bus drivers had gone on strike. 'What could be the reason?' he wondered. He walked over to his friend Mohan's place. After exchanging pleasantries, Hamid asked why the bus employees had declared a strike. Mohan informed him that the trade union had demanded a raise, but the company owners had not bothered, hence the strike. 'That's quite reassuring,' Hamid said, impressed. 'The workers of this country are starting to show such courage. It speaks of their awareness. Why do I think you had a hand in this?' Mohan smiled. 'Well, Naseeruddin, who leads the Sindhi union, deserves most of the credit. I played a small part. He is a bright young man.'

'The company owners will have to give in to this pressure. They will continue to incur losses if the buses don't function,' Hamid said.

'Let them recognise the power of labour. They must learn to value the labourers and realise that they don't have a choice but to appreciate them,' Mohan said.

'Now let them see that the seed of unrest lies in the economic context, not in a religious one. Some employees must be Hindu, some Muslim. At times like these, who thinks of being one or the other? What matters are the essential needs, which are common to both. Does it matter whether the owners are Hindus or Muslims?' Hamid said.

'Of course, hunger and unemployment are caused by capitalists, not by *jaati* differences. It is the owners who give them a religious colouring and instigate one group against the other. They take advantage of the helplessness and illiteracy of the labourers,' Mohan concurred.

Hamid responded, '*Bilkul theek*. At least where there is unity among labourers against the capitalists, there will be no possibility of communal strife. It is these elite and the middlemen who instigate Hindu and Muslim differences. In reality, there is no religious strife between a poor Hindu and a poor Muslim.'

'This foreign government stands to gain from creating this strife. If only we had our own state... You know, it's the people from the Muslim League and the Hindu Mahasabha who make things worse. I believe that we need a socialist state of our own—neither Hindu nor Muslim will become hegemonic,' Hamid said.

'Of course, money is the root of all problems. If the means of production were handed over to ordinary people, nobody would dare disturb them. It's infuriating that those who produce food do not have food, and those who create cloth go around naked. What an unjust situation this is!' Mohan said.

'I believe that a communist state will solve some of these minor problems. Once the proletariat takes charge, nobody will acquire dominance, and minor skirmishes will not be fanned,' Hamid said.

'Friend, the truth is, even religion is an intoxication. The rich people use this tool to mislead the poor,' Mohan said softly.

'Yes, of course. That's what I like about Russia. It has set a good example of driving out religion and addressing unemployment and poverty,' Hamid said.

'Friend, I hear that you are headed towards Russia. Is that true?'

'Yes,' Hamid replied. 'At least, that's the plan.'

'You're so fortunate! All eyes are on Russia now. It has become the ideal for many young people. It seems to be the only model that can uproot deep-seated class differences, as well as petty caste and religious distinctions, and provide a life of dignity and honour. There is a scientific and educated way of doing things there. I hope I get a chance to go there someday. Anyway, tell me, when are you going to Lucknow?' Mohan asked.

'Very soon. This month has been so enriching. Being with you has made my stay so much better.'

'Sindh needs people like you. Muslims like you will lead Sindh through this difficult period towards more progressive thinking,' Mohan said.

'Our Sindh is going to set an example of Sufi thought, of equality, and of *ittehad* between the two communities,' Hamid added.

'Ameen,' Mohan said.

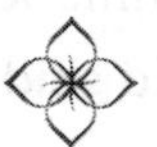

21

Hamid had requested a six-month leave from his college authorities, and within a month, his leave was granted. He organised his passport and booked his passage to Russia. In short, he was all set to go. But his heart was full of misgivings. While it was exciting to visit Russia, he could not stop thinking about Asha. How could he leave without wishing her goodbye? Would she not take it amiss if he left without saying anything? He wondered how she was doing. She had not written to him, but then again, neither had he. Should he go visit her? Then it occurred to him that he could visit Vijay and ask him after Asha. After all, it was only expected that he would say goodbye to his friend; otherwise, Aruna would not let him hear the end of it. They will be happy to see him, and it would be nice to catch up with them before he undertook such a long journey.

Hamid prepared to leave for Allahabad. He boarded the train with a suitcase and bedding in hand. The journey seemed inexorably long. Although Hamid was generally patient, he felt restless this time. He took a taxi from Allahabad station and headed straight to Vijay's house. Aruna was coming out of the house when she saw Hamid. 'Surprise! Astonished to see me, right? Is Vijay not home?' Hamid smiled.

'Oh, he'll be here any moment,' Aruna said.

'Is he alright? I have not heard from him in ages!' Hamid said.

'He's just so engrossed in his newspaper. He was working until 2 am yesterday. Plus, there's other stuff to look after. By the way, we are leaving tonight,' Aruna said.

'Where are you going?'

'Almora.'

'Is everything okay? *Sab khairiyat*?' Hamid's heart skipped a beat.

'Asha's mother is unwell. In fact, she's quite critical.'

'Oh my God! She must be all alone there.'

'She knows many people there. She was quite well when she stayed with us, but suddenly, her intestines became weak. We gave her only fluids and fruit juice for a month. She simply could not digest any food. Asha thought she might be missing Almora. The doctor also mentioned that Allahabad's weather might not suit her; she should go to a colder place. So, Vijay left both mother and daughter there. While it seemed that she was recovering, last night we received Asha's letter stating that her mother's condition had worsened.'

'Poor Asha! It's barely been six months since she lost her father, and now her mother is in this condition. She must be so heartbroken. There is no escaping death.'

'Death is not just inevitable but also desirable, don't you think?' Aruna asked. 'Who would value life if there was no death?'

'True, but at least science has managed to address minor illnesses that used to be the cause of death in the past.'

'Anyway, let's not talk about morbid things. Tell me about yourself,' Aruna changed the topic.

'What should I say about myself? You've given me such disturbing news. I feel very bad for Asha. God forbid, if her mother dies, what will she do? She has only one parent left now.'

'That's what Vijay and I were discussing yesterday. Oh, here he comes!'

Vijay's face lit up on seeing Hamid. The two embraced each other.

'Hamid, what brought you here? Please tell me you missed me.'

Hamid laughed. 'That is the truth. But you wouldn't have believed it, so I didn't say it.'

'Oh, come on! Tell me, what are your other reasons?'

'Actually, there are many other reasons. I also came to say goodbye before leaving.'

'Now where are you off to? You've become quite the wanderer!'

'Russia,' Hamid replied.

'Do you actually think you'll be able to make Hindustan a communist country by going to Russia?'

'You have a point, my friend. But what can I do? Nature has made me different from you. I am an incorrigible optimist. So I am hoping that the universe has something in store for me, and one way or another, I will be able to make a difference. If the universe finds me capable, it will make me her instrument. Just pray for that to happen.' Hamid responded politely.

Hamid's words were so earnest that Vijay felt small and silly for saying the superficial things he had. He asked Hamid, 'Are you sure about going?'

'As sure as one can be of anything. The rest is up to Allah.'

22

The moment Hamid reached Lucknow, he wrote Asha a letter.

Asha,

I understand that you must be upset with me. Guilty as charged. Despite thinking about it constantly, I don't know why I haven't written sooner. I was deeply disturbed to learn about your beloved mother's illness. Qadir's ways are strange, as they say. We have no choice but to accept His will. If we don't learn how to swim in the ocean of life, we'll be swallowed by the waves. A skilled practiced swimmer does not like still waters, and we need to emulate such swimmers. There's pleasure in a choppy sea if we stop resisting.

Vijay must have told you that I am headed to Russia. I intend to leave India on 1st November, but

I need your consent. I am pining for you and don't know if I will be fortunate enough to see you before I leave. I also don't know if that will be enough. I am surviving, but also hoping.

Khuda hafiz.

Yours,
Hamid

After what seemed like an endless wait, Hamid received Asha's reply.

Hamid,
Gifts come on unexpected days. At a time when my heart was torn to pieces, it was precisely this letter that I needed. My beloved mother has passed away, leaving behind this unreal world. Dust has returned to dust. I know this is inevitable, but I am finding it difficult to live without her. A mother is precious to a daughter. I realise that only now.

Your letter brought much consolation. I wish I could become your disciple. How well you write! You have asked me for my consent, but what if my heart cannot give you permission to leave? You can go as far away as you like from my sight, but what am I to do about my heart that longs to be with you?

May you keep well.

Your Asha

Hamid felt greatly comforted upon receiving Asha's letter. He was certainly saddened by the news of Gauri Devi's death, but the joy of hearing from Asha outweighed the sadness. It was clear that he did not have Asha's consent to go to Russia. Now what was to be done? He had already made all the arrangements for his travel. Asha's despondent face haunted him. How could he leave her in this condition? While he was still mulling over this matter, he heard the postman call out. There was a telegram from Vijay, asking him to immediately come to Allahabad.

Hamid arrived at Allahabad station and saw Vijay waiting there. He asked him why he had been called to Allahabad so suddenly. Vijay replied softly that it was Asha's desire.

'When do you plan to leave for Russia?' Vijay asked.

'On 1st November,' Hamid answered. His heart began to pound.

'Asha is quite depressed. She has lost both parents in such a short time and feels very lonely and orphaned. We are trying our best to cheer her up, but we know it's not effective. She is not saying much, and that is to be expected. She is that kind of a person; she does not show her emotions easily. Aruna says that she sobs in her bed all night. She feels like there is no one she can call her own. She managed to get over her father's death but is finding it difficult to accept her mother's passing.'

'I understand. A mother means everything to a daughter. At the moment, her only comfort is you and Aruna. She will also find some comfort in Shantiniketan.'

'Our affection alone is not enough, and I highly doubt that art and poetry at Shantiniketan will help right now. Women need something more at times like this.'

Hamid understood the underlying meaning in Vijay's words. He did not think it appropriate to say anything more.

They reached home. Hamid's heart ached to see Asha. She belonged to him now. It was an overwhelming feeling. He found her sitting on a sofa, reading a Hindi novel. She was startled to see Hamid. When he sat down close to her, her eyes filled with tears. Was she feeling joy or despair, only she knew, but her guard collapsed. What she had managed to hide from everyone else, she could no longer conceal. Hamid gently ran his fingers through her hair.

'Asha, I have faith in your courage. I know your grief is enormous, but you are also not an ordinary person. Why should you need someone else's consolation?' Hamid wiped her tears with his handkerchief. 'Asha, how can I go on living, knowing you are so unhappy? It's killing me. Tell me, how can I help you?'

Hamid's touch made Asha dizzy with exhilaration. She merely looked at him silently, as if her eyes were saying something. Hamid's heart filled with love for her.

'Asha, do you want me to abandon my plans to go to Russia?'

'Tell me, who are you leaving me with? What support?' Asha wept.

'Would you like to come with me?' Hamid looked into her eyes.

'Only if you don't mind...'

'Alright, leave everything to me then,' Hamid said determinedly. Asha lowered her head. Hamid became quiet. There was nothing more to be said.

23

It was Asha and Hamid's wedding day. Hamid had given two weeks' notice to the magistrate's office and, in the meantime, arranged for Asha's passport and tickets. He had also informed his parents about his forthcoming wedding. Today, he received a telegram from his parents congratulating him. However, what gave him even more joy was a telegram from Mohan: 'Best wishes to you on your marriage. May you find happiness and self-realisation with your life partner. Mohini and I rejoice in your happiness. We also got married yesterday and deserve to be congratulated by you!'

Hamid's joy knew no bounds. He was very impressed by this couple's integrity and love. He narrated their story to Aruna.

'That's so beautiful. Remarriage is incredibly important for women. It allows them to rebuild their lives and find hope anew. Love has the power to bring so much joy to them.'

24

When Hamid and Asha had signed their marriage papers at the magistrate's office, their hearts were content. They had chosen each other. Hearts bound by mutual love and understanding are like the meeting of the Ganga and the Jamuna. What caste, religion, or difference can stand in the way of such a spiritual partnership?

As Shah Abdul Latif says,

'There was neither care nor a difference of you and I.

There was only joy in the heart, and before, the face of the beloved.'

25

Vijay and Aruna were jubilant. Aruna hugged Asha and said, ‘Behan, you have been a worshipper of nature, and that’s why nature has been partial to you. All your wishes have come true.’ Vijay congratulated Hamid and quietly placed a sealed envelope in his hand, saying, ‘Here’s your wedding present. Please accept it.’ Hamid opened the envelope. Its contents surprised him. It contained the will and testament of the late Shankarlal.

Shankarlal had died suddenly, leaving behind neither an inheritance nor a letter. According to Hindu laws of inheritance, as the only surviving male member, Vijay was entitled to inherit everything from Shankarlal. As such, he was in charge of everything that Shankarlal had left behind. Vijay had undertaken the responsibility of Asha’s care and education. He was far too just to desire his own share in Shankarlal’s property. He handed over everything to Asha, who was the rightful inheritor, if not legally, but certainly morally.

Hamid's hands shook as he held the documents. He returned the envelope to Vijay, saying, 'Your generosity is almost embarrassing to me, but I do not wish to own this property. I do not consider myself a successor to Shankarlal's wealth. It is not justifiable from any point of view. In any case, I can only lay claim to what I earn through love and labour. I am also acutely aware that Shankarlal would not have accepted me as his son-in-law. All the more reason why I should have nothing to do with his wealth. In fact, I believe that Asha should not claim it either. She will have to adjust to my source of livelihood, but I cannot force her beyond a point. It is her autonomy. I will say this though, my sense of male honour would suffer a setback if I were to accept this. And I believe that I have enough honour of my own not to want to enhance it by this inappropriate possession.'

Vijay looked at Hamid's face, stupefied. 'Hamid, you are a marvel! At a time when young men are chasing the mirage of money and getting embroiled in it to the extent of compromising their ethics and self-respect, you remain so indifferent to this *maya*. But listen, I, too, have a conscience. I will not usurp an orphan girl's property. It is against my principles. I would like to hand over to Asha what rightfully belongs to her. Since you will take care of Asha, it is only legitimate that you take care of this enormous property.'

Asha was listening to this exchange between Vijay and Hamid. At this point, she intervened, 'This property belongs to the underprivileged.' Hamid was delighted to hear this and immediately said with enthusiasm, 'That's brilliant! Vijay, we leave this property under your care. Please start something—a workshop, a factory—that can provide employment, housing, and schooling to the poor. And you must take a share for your own labour that will go into establishing and expanding this project.'

'*Arre wah*, Hamid! There can be no better *dharam* or *karam* than this—no religion or deed is superior to this. This is also your dream of an egalitarian society come true. Your little experiment will set an example for capitalist sharks.'

Aruna commented, 'This is so ironic. Who would have thought that a staunch Hindu like Shankarlal, who avoided even the shadow of a Muslim, would have a close Muslim relative? And who would have thought that the real inheritors of Shankarlal's wealth, accrued by exploiting the poor, would be the poor themselves!'

26

After his marriage, Hamid sent telegrams to all his relatives, friends, and well-wishers, and within no time, he was inundated with telegrams congratulating him. His parents sent their blessings in an extremely affectionate letter. Hamid sent them a photograph from the day of the wedding. Even those who did not approve of this inter-religious marriage did not dare to utter a word. The firmness and solidarity with which Hamid's parents stood by him did not allow tongues to wag. Umed Ali's guru, Pir saheb also sent his blessings. His letter was eloquent and heartfelt: 'You have heralded a universe of unions. Your *ittehad* is not merely physical or emotional, but spiritual. When hearts marry each other, no force in the world can separate them.' Hamid and Asha were overcome with joy and gratitude.

Meanwhile, Hamid and Asha thought of returning to his parents' home instead of going away on a honeymoon. But before that, there was something else that claimed

Hamid's attention. He was worried about his sister, Zarina. Hamid knew that once he was gone, Zarina's life would be dictated by parental and Islamic norms, leaving her no room to develop her independent spirit. Hamid was very attached to his sister, and every time he saw her beautiful face, he prayed for a progressive and fulfilling life for her. He was not going to be a witness to the process of consigning her to a religious or patriarchal orthodoxy. If Vijay and Aruna had managed to rescue Asha from a bigoted Hindu home, surely he and Asha could play an equally encouraging role in Zarina's life.

These were Hamid's thoughts, which he had not yet shared with Asha. Finally, one night, Hamid broached the subject with her. He was convinced that she would support him, so he told her, 'Asha, I carry a burden inside me, and I feel only you can help lift it from my heart.' Asha was deeply moved and replied, 'Hamid, I have been so keen to do something for you. I keep wondering what I could possibly do. How can I make myself worthy of your love? How will I ever forget what you have done for me? You injected life into my deadened heart. There was little difference between living and dying; that's how passive my life was. I consider myself a confident and strong Indian woman today because you gave me the space to grow. Please tell me what I can do for you so that I can find something to offer in return.' Hamid was overwhelmed by Asha's words. He kissed her gently and said, 'Please extend love and encouragement to Zarina.

Make her your own. If she's away from my parents' influence and stays under our supervision, she may flourish and become an independent person.'

Asha immediately replied, 'In that case, your sister is my sister, too. All those who are yours are mine as well. I will not let any desire of mine get in the way. I am happy to have her as part of our family.'

Hamid expressed his relief, 'That's great! Let's impress upon Amma and Baba that their son has not been snatched away from them, rather, he cares for his sister and is ready to take on her responsibility. They have been generous and gracious to me and stood by me in all my decisions. They will also see why we are together, that we share the same values and ethics.'

Asha said, 'If you have faith in my love, then leave the rest to me. I don't want to say more. I am not good at expressing myself with words. I want you to see for yourself when the time comes.' Asha looked into Hamid's eyes. They were both quiet. They had made a long journey and now knew that the love that had drawn them together came from a deep place—a place not bound by any creed or caste.

27

As the train approached Karachi, Asha felt a knot of tension in her body. She had been praying all night, hoping that Hamid's family would welcome her. Hamid, on the other hand, was fully confident that his parents' love was unwavering. The train pulled into the station. Asha looked out of the window and saw the eager faces of Umed Ali, Roshan Ara, Gulu, and Zarina. Her fears began to melt away. Asha and Hamid alighted from the train and lowered their heads to seek blessings from Hamid's parents. Hamid said to his mother, 'Amma, this is Asha. She wouldn't even go on a honeymoon. She was not interested in Europe or Russia. Instead, she wanted to come and meet all of you.' Roshan Ara embraced Asha and kissed her forehead. Umed Ali placed his hand on her head and blessed her. As for Gulu and Zarina, they clung to their brother and his wife like creepers. The car headed home.

Asha set foot in her new home. Roshan Ara had decorated a bedroom for the newly-wed couple. Every wall and corner was decked with fresh flowers. The room had new furniture, and festoons hung from the ceiling. All the fears and differences faded away, such were the waves of affection. Asha had not expected to receive so much respect and warmth.

When they sat down to eat at the dining table, Hamid said to his father, 'Baba, we don't have to live apart from each other anymore. However, it will take some planning before we can start living together. Here's what I suggest: I will need to spend a few years in London and accomplish certain tasks. I am working on a couple of books and need to get them published. We also don't know what kind of times India will witness now. You know how Jinnah *saheb* has been thinking and what his ideological bent is. I don't want to live in Pakistan. Given how Sufi you have been, and how broadminded Amma is, even you will find it difficult to live in Pakistan. Also, Amma will not be able to live without me. I am sure that India's freedom will come at a heavy price, and Partition is inevitable. I would want you to live with me. I want to live in India. I consider myself an Indian. I will not leave you alone in Pakistan and certainly not alone at this stage of life. I don't want our family to be divided, so I would like all of us to live in Delhi. I suggest you sell this house and send the money to Vijay. I have written to both Vijay and Aruna, and they will come here in a week's time to meet you. I have asked them to look for a good house for us in Delhi and purchase it. If, for the sake of staying with me and also keeping in mind the children's education, you sell this house in Karachi at this stage, you will get a good price. Meanwhile, Asha and I will take Zarina with us to London. You can see that Zarina refuses to leave Asha's side. Moreover, Ranjit and his father are moving to London because Ranjit wants to earn his science degree there. You, Amma and Gulu join me in London. Once things settle down, we will all stay together in Delhi.' Umed Ali listened to his son carefully and agreed with the plan.

28

Aruna and Vijay joined the family in a few days. They all spent time discussing the future course of action. There was great trust and understanding between them all. Asha, in particular, had won everyone's hearts. Her mother-in-law had begun to value her opinion and treated her like her own daughter. Asha said to Roshan Ara, 'Amma, we will take Zarina with us. She and I will both study the social sciences, and our education will help us contribute to the nascent nation. Aruna and Vijay have already taught me English, and my parents taught me Hindi and Sanskrit. With some additional exposure in London, I will be able to participate in social work. Having Zarina with us will be really good for me as well. I don't want you to worry about her. Please trust me on this.' Asha's voice carried conviction and love, making it difficult not to be drawn by such power.

Hamid received a letter from Mohan. He and Mohini had gone on a holiday to Ooty and Mysore. They promised to return before Hamid left for London. Mohan mentioned that he was very eager to meet Asha. If a woman had managed to make Hamid fall in love, she must be special. He remembered that Asha liked to recite shlokas from the Gita, so he and Mohini had bought a statue of Lord Krishna made of sandalwood. Looking at Krishna playing the flute reminded them of Asha's melodic voice. Hamid told Asha how committed Mohan was to the unity of Hindus and Muslims, and how Mohan intended to work with communist principles in Sindh. Asha could not wait to meet him.

When Asha, Aruna, and Mohini got together under the same roof, it was like a galaxy of the new women of India. They were strong, committed feminists who had no patience with religious superstitions and institutions that kept women oppressed. Asha's weapons were not external; she was deeply influenced by Gandhi, and therefore, she used love to win her battles.

29

Within the next two months, Hamid had managed to find a house in London. His parents and Gulu joined him. Zarina and Asha had begun their education at a college there, and Gulu was admitted to a school. Hamid spent four years in London. He already knew many people there. Roshan Ara and Umed Ali were happier in London than in Karachi. They were surrounded by their loved ones, so they did not miss their own country. Ranjit's father was also nearby, and the two families met regularly. The backdrop of the Second World War did create some fear and insecurity, but everyone relied upon Hamid's wisdom and foresight and somehow managed to remain calm. Umed Ali immersed himself in writing a book on Sufism. The war ended, and they were happy about the defeat of fascism.

Zarina and Ranjit grew closer to each other, and their parents happily agreed to a civil marriage between them. Ranjit said to Zarina, 'Now I believe in God. I had asked for you, and I have you now.' Zarina replied, 'Yes, I do believe our Allah and Ishwar had some role to play. There was a time when it seemed our parents would never agree, but look how supportive they have become.'

Ranjit's aunt lived in Bombay. She was a widow and lived all alone in a large apartment. She wrote to her brother, suggesting that Ranjit and Zarina could stay with her and establish a career there. Gulu had spent every day with his sister and asked his brother and parents if he could stay with her and Ranjit in Bombay.

Meanwhile, Hamid planned to come to Delhi with Asha and his parents. Gandhi was assassinated that year, making him and Asha feel extremely disheartened. However, he also had a lot of faith in Nehru. As for Asha, she wanted to raise her child in independent India, not in a country that had colonised India. So, they all returned to India and began to live in a house that Vijay had already set up for them. Hamid and Asha's child was born there. Asha named him Satprem, the love(r) of truth, as a special tribute to Gandhi. She immersed herself in the rehabilitation of refugees and helped both Hindus and Muslims affected by Partition.

Hamid was given many new assignments by Nehru and became busy with the reconstruction of a new India under the Nehruvian vision. Meanwhile, Umed Ali had managed to acquire one of the famous wooden *pingos* from Sindh. When the grandparents rocked Satprem in the swing, they felt close to Sindh and believed they were nurturing a child born of Sufi heritage. They sang a lullaby for him:

'May you be the light of truth.
May Sindh live through you.'